The WednesdaY Wizard

Mother Wyse's eyes turned to glowing slits and she looked very grave and grim. "I hope you're stronger than you look, Weasel," she croaked, "because you're going to need all the strength you have."

Denzil gulped and backed away. "What do you mean?" he asked.

"A dragon, that's what I mean," she said, leaning forward and jabbing her bony finger at his chest. "You are in mortal danger, Weasel. I had a dream of the near future – a dream of strangeness and fear and violent death."

Other titles in the Hippo Fantasy series:

Rowan of Rin
Emily Rodda

The Night of Wishes
Michael Ende

Watch out for:

The Practical Princess
Jay Williams

Ratspell
Paddy Mounter

Hippo Fantasy

The WednesdaY Wizard

Sherryl Jordan

Scholastic Children's Books,
Scholastic Publications Ltd,
7–9 Pratt Street, London NW1 0AE, UK

Scholastic Inc.,
555 Broadway, New York, NY 10012-3999, USA

Scholastic Canada Ltd,
123 Newkirk Road, Richmond Hill,
Ontario, Canada L4C 3G5

Ashton Scholastic Pty Ltd,
P O Box 579, Gosford, New South Wales,
Australia

Ashton Scholastic Ltd,
Private Bag 92801, Penrose, Auckland,
New Zealand

First published by Ashton Scholastic, New Zealand, 1991

First published in the UK by Scholastic Publications Ltd, 1993

This edition, 1994

Text copyright © Sherryl Jordan, 1991

ISBN 0 590 55644 4

Typeset in Palatino by TW Typesetting, Midsomer Norton, Avon
Printed by Cox & Wyman Ltd, Reading, Berks.

10 9 8 7 6 5 4 3 2 1

Contents

Chapter 1

The Witch's Warning

Denzil never meant to be a thief. He'd been told that doing wicked things lessened his special powers, and weakened the magic in him. Also, he knew that thieves, if caught, had their hands chopped off. So he called himself a burglar – it sounded more honourable, more daring. The word burglar had a grand ring to it, if you said it right. But there was something sneaky about the word thief, something little and mean. Denzil was never a thief. He wasn't wicked either, and the last thing he wanted to do was to weaken his magic powers. But sometimes, on rare occasions, it was necessary for him to be a burglar. And such a time was this.

His master, Valvasor, had been away for several weeks now, and Denzil was desperate for some proper food. In particular, he was desperate for honey and hedgehog pie. The hedgehog part wasn't difficult – hedgehogs were all over the place – but the honey was a problem. Valvasor's honeypot was empty, and had been since the day he left, when Denzil had eaten the lot for morning tea. Nor was there any to buy at the village market. The only place to get honey was where Mother Wyse lived. She kept bees (among other dangerous things) and her honey was famous all over the land. It was pure gold – gold and clear like summer skies – and sweet. Sweet, so sweet. Denzil's mouth dribbled at the memory of it.

He wiped his lips on his grubby sleeve and crept closer to Mother Wyse's cottage. He could see her far away across the fields, her robes black against the early morning light. She was bent double, gathering poisonous plants, and Denzil knew she'd be gone a long time yet. It would take her until midday to walk back, she was so old, slow and weak. She was deaf and short-sighted, too, and wouldn't have known he was there even if he was wearing bright red and roaring like a bull. Nevertheless, he moved quietly, from habit, and even a hawk would have had trouble seeing him against the earth, he was so dirty, drab and brown. He pushed open the low cottage door, ducked his head, and went in.

The cottage had only one room, and it was grimier than Denzil. Every time he moved, clouds of dust rose in the dim air. There were no windows in the cottage, and the only light came from the fire that flickered in a pit in the dirt floor. A pitch-black cat sat beside the fire, watching Denzil with gleaming yellow eyes. He left the door wide open, letting in a thin ray of sunshine, and looked around.

Mother Wyse's home hadn't changed since the time Valvasor had brought him here six winters ago. He had been very small then – so small he hadn't been able to see the things on her table. The place didn't look as big now as it had then, and it seemed less threatening. But still it was like something out of a bad dream. There were mangy animal skins hanging on the walls, covering gaps in the stone where the wind whistled in. There were wooden cages piled in one corner and filled with small living animals: squirrels and stoats, lizards and toads, and one tiny monkey with a wizened face like a sad old man's. There were shelves of bottles, bowls, carved boxes, dried plants, stuffed animals, and grinning human skulls.

Magic hung in the air like a dark mist. It haunted the shadows, half-seen shapes deep in the smoky shelves, and it glinted in strange poisons and in the glass eyes of stuffed animals. And there were books too, shelves and shelves of books.

Valvasor doesn't need books, thought Denzil smugly. He has everything inside his head. He's full right up with magic. It hangs on him like a cloak, oozes out of his fingernails, he breathes it out . . . even his shadow falling on a clay bird can make it come alive. He doesn't need books. He's the highest and the best wizard in the world. And he's teaching it all to me.

Denzil sauntered over to one of the shelves, and began sniffing in jars and bowls, looking for honey. He found a jar of all kinds of loose teeth, probably from animals, and a bowl of glowing coloured stones. He discovered a box of human hair, beautifully plaited, and a stone jar of strangely shaped pickles. But there was no honey.

He went over to one of the skins hanging on the back wall, lifted it, and peered out through a wide crack. Mother Wyse was still far away, pulling plants and roots from the damp earth. He could tell it was her because a black crow flew around her head. Old Battybird the villagers called her, because of that crow. Denzil had called her Battybird once, and Valvasor had smacked his ear.

Dropping the skin, Denzil turned back to the room. Now, where was the honey? There was a low bench of cooking things, and he searched it thoroughly, throwing dried herbs onto the dusty floor, and overturning bowls and plates. He picked up a bowl that had blackberries soaking in it, and sniffed it.

Suddenly the cottage door banged shut, plunging the room into darkness. Denzil yelped and dropped the bowl, which shattered on his toe. He spun round, breathless with pain and terror. He could see nothing but the red glow of the dying fire, the cat's eyes shining, and countless pitch-black shadows, all moving.

Slowly, a shadow darker than the rest left its place by the door and moved to the fire. The shadow bent over, puffing and muttering, and poked the embers into life. The flames flared up, and bright light flashed across a sharp, cunning face, masses of tangled hair, and eyes like red coals burning.

Mother Wyse!

Astounded, Denzil backed away. How did she get back so fast?

Mother Wyse looked at him, her face screwed up in a thoughtful frown. "You're Weasel, aren't you?" she croaked, scratching her whiskery chin. "Valvasor's boy."

Denzil nodded. His throat was dry, and his heart banged like a drum. He tried to think quickly. "He – Valvasor sent me," he lied.

Mother Wyse lifted a shaggy eyebrow, and her one tooth glimmered in the firelight. "Did he now?" she cackled.

"Yes. He needs . . . um . . ."

"Bleeds, did you say?" she asked sharply. "Bleeds? Is he hurt?"

"No! *Needs*," said Denzil loudly. "He *needs* a dried bat's wing. He's making a spell."

"A fried fat thing?" said Mother Wyse, going over to her cages. She took out a plump toad, went back to the fire, and held the startled animal by one leg over a red-hot log.

"No!" yelled Denzil. "*A dried bat's wing!* He's making spells!"

"Why didn't you say so then?" muttered Mother Wyse, hobbling away and shoving the toad back into its cage. "Got plenty of those. How many does he want? Not just one, surely. He needs more than one if he's taking them in cockle shells."

"Ten," said Denzil.

Mother Wyse went over to a cluttered shelf, poked around among the skulls and stuffed squirrels, and came back with a carved box. She stood close to Denzil and lifted the lid. "Take ten then," she said, leaning towards him. She was so close he could smell the fresh spring grass in her clothes, and the deeper smell of wild herbs. She didn't look so scary close up. He saw that she was very thin, her cheeks were sunken and hollow, and there were whiskers up her nose. He was taller than she was.

He swallowed nervously and put his fingers into the box. He felt leathery wings, paper-thin. One at a time, he pulled out ten, and placed them into his other hand. "Thank you, Mother," he said, hoping he sounded grateful. "He can finish the spells, now."

"You're a bad liar, Weasel," said Mother Wyse, softly. "About as bad at lying as you are at thieving."

For a moment Denzil looked nonplussed; then he lifted his chin, and his eyes flashed. "I'm not a thief!" he said haughtily, stuffing the bats' wings into his pocket and wishing they were honeycomb. "I'm a burglar. There's a difference. And I'm Denzil, not Weasel."

"I do beg your pardon," she murmured. She looked at him hard, her eyes narrowed. She saw the proud tilt of his head, and the way his nostrils flared when he was angry. His eyes were a strange green, pale and clear like glass. They shone like fire beneath his black brows and through his wild black hair. He was filthy, thin, and tall for his age.

He must be ten now, she thought, frowning, trying to remember. Ten years it would have been since old Valvasor had told her that a ragged bundle of bones had been left on his doorstep. A baby whose mother couldn't afford to look after him; a baby with long, wild hair even then, and eyes full of ancient wisdom and light. And Valvasor had kept him and brought him up, and was training him in wizardly ways. He was doing a good job, too, though the boy wasn't disciplined enough. Hot-headed, this child was – hot-headed, stubborn, bold and wild. And, she remembered suddenly, he was in grave danger.

"I'm glad you've come, Weasel," she said, urgently. "I've got news for you. What are you like at fighting dragons?"

Denzil blinked, taken aback. Then he shrugged. "Never had any practice," he said. "I fought a fox once. And a bear." He hesitated.

"A giant, too," he added for good measure.

Mother Wyse's eyes turned to glowing slits and she looked very grave and grim. "I hope you're stronger than you look, Weasel," she croaked, "because you're going to need all the strength you have."

Denzil gulped and backed away. "What do you mean?" he asked.

"A dragon, that's what I mean," she said, leaning forward and jabbing her bony finger at his chest. "You are in mortal danger, Weasel. I had a dream of the near future – a dream of strangeness and fear and violent death.

"Are you listening, Weasel? It is a dream of you. A dream of you in a strange, big town. Of you in this town at night, full of dark and dread and rushing things, and behold! A dragon comes – a long black dragon, with one eye blazing gold, and claws stretched out far, far to get you – and it rushes, roaring – and – ah, Weasel! I cannot tell the end! But I warn you, I warn you! Beware! Beware of a big town on

11

Spy Wednesday. Spy Wednesday it is, when the dragon comes. Spy Wednesday is the day the dream foretold."

Denzil went white, and his whole world spun with terrible whirling fear. Mother Wyse gripped his shirt and leaned so close that he felt the hot wind of her breath on his face. "Beware of Spy Wednesday!" she hissed. "Beware of the large town! And, Weasel, most of all, beware of the dragon!"

Trying hard to think, and not to panic, Denzil stuttered, "But I'm not in a big town. And Spy Wednesday's only four days away."

"Aye, it is," she breathed, nodding.

"But even if I ran like a rabbit, I wouldn't be in a big town by Spy Wednesday," said Denzil, pulling free of her, and straightening his shirt. "I can't possibly be in a big town by Spy Wednesday. You're wrong! You've got everything mixed up. Nothing's going to happen to me. On Spy Wednesday I'll still be in my own little village waiting for Valvasor.

No dragon's going to get me! You're wrong!"

Angry now for being so frightened for nothing, he strode over to the door and pulled it open. Sunlight poured into the dim room. He blinked in the glare, feeling the sun's warmth and power, and realized that the room had been very cold. He stepped out into the light, glad to escape.

"Beware!" Mother Wyse shrieked after him. "Beware!"

But he laughed and ran down the hillside, feeling the long grass warm and soft beneath his bare feet, and the bright joy of spring like a song all around. He ran all the way back to the tiny village and fished in the stream for his dinner, and forgot all about her warning.

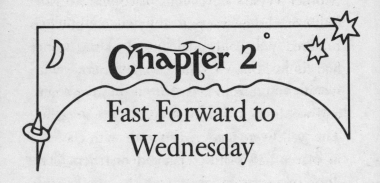

Chapter 2

Fast Forward to Wednesday

Denzil sat on Valvasor's huge bed and ate his fish. He wasn't a good cook, and most of the flesh was still raw. There were a few scales still on it, too.

"Ages and ages," he muttered, spitting out a bone. "Ages and ages before he's back to do the cooking. I'll starve before then." He sighed, and put his clay bowl on the floor under the bed, next to the dirty bowls from the last nine meals. He'd have to do the washing-up soon, or he'd run out of dishes.

He sighed again, and looked around the home

he shared with the wizard. Compared with Mother Wyse's hovel, this place was a castle. Valvasor's home was practically new – only two hundred years old – and none of the stones had tumbled down. There were windows with wooden shutters to keep out the wind and rain, and woollen curtains to keep out the draughts. The walls were plastered smooth with clay and in places had pictures painted on them. The floor, made from great wooden planks, was scattered with thick furs for comfort and warmth. There was a proper stone fireplace with a stone funnel to take the smoke out through a hole in the roof. Valvasor had invented that funnel, last year. It saved them from having to sit in clouds of smoke all the time.

There was no kitchen. Like everyone else in the village, they cooked over the fire and washed their dishes and cooking-pots in the stream. There was no bathroom because they'd never heard of baths, and the toilet was a hole in the ground outside. The only bed was Valvasor's, and it was so hard and uncomfortable that Denzil wouldn't sleep in it. He preferred to sleep on the hearth, wrapped in a fur. While the wizard was away Denzil did use the bed to sit on though, because it was softer than the wooden stools, and it was handy to put dirty dishes under.

There were shelves and huge carved cupboards, and all Valvasor's things were kept neat and tidy – except when he was away of course. The place was a bit of a pigsty now, but Denzil had ages in which to clean it up. Valvasor was away in London Town, where he'd spend weeks wandering around the markets, performing marvels for the townsfolk, and visiting old friends. In the meantime, Denzil could be as untidy as he liked. And he liked untidiness very much.

The table where he and Valvasor worked, usually polished and tidy, was littered now with bowls and leather bottles, pieces of plants, mushrooms, dead moths and butterflies, feathers, strange stones, used cups, apple cores, mouldy crusts, and an old sock with a family of mice in it. There were a few books open on the table. They contained the only magic Valvasor had ever written down, and were supposed to be for Denzil when he was older. But he had been reading them while his master was away, and making all the spells Valvasor had forbidden. He'd made a good job of most of them, too, especially the ones that changed things to new shapes.

Denzil lay back on the bed, smiling, his hands linked behind his head, and thought of all the marvellous things he had made. He'd never had so much fun in his life. Or been so worried, at times. The best thing he'd made was a small dragon. Out of clay he'd formed it, then worked strong magic into it, and made it come alive. The dragon was only small, about the size of Denzil's foot, and it had run round the room tripping over furs and falling into the fireplace – fortunately, when the fire was out. Denzil had put it in a bowl to wash the ashes off, and it had learned to swim. It was so good at swimming that Denzil even let it swim in the big cauldron of soup, before it got too hot.

Then the dragon discovered it had wings, and had flown around the room, so excited that it breathed fire and set the thatched roof alight. That had been one of the worrying times.

Denzil had got the fire under control eventually, and had stolen a whole bag of gold to pay the thatcher to replace the demolished roof. He'd paid him a second stolen bagful as well, just to keep his mouth shut when Valvasor came home. The dragon had disappeared, but sometimes Denzil heard flutterings like bats at night, and suspected he heard something licking the bowls under the bed. He hoped that if it was the dragon, its fire had run out.

Bothersome animals, dragons, he thought. And then he remembered the dragon Mother Wyse had warned him of.

"Silly old crow," he muttered, aloud. "She doesn't know what she's talking about. How could I possibly be in a big town by Spy Wednesday? She's always mixed up. Because she's deaf, I s'pose. Valvasor's the one in a big town, not me. He's the one who ought to look out for dreadful things and dragons, not me. He's the one . . ."

Denzil sat up suddenly, his face white. "Valvasor!" he cried. "She must have meant Valvasor! He's the one in danger, not me!"

He jumped up and raced over to the table. He tore a page out of a book, grabbed a feather quill, and dipped it in the inkwell. "BEE CAIR-FULL!" he wrote, in large shaky letters. "A DRAGON WILL TRI TO KILL YOO. MOTHER WYZZ SED."

He stopped, gnawing the end of the quill, frowning. He'd run out of paper, and he hadn't even mentioned Spy Wednesday.

"It's no use!" he groaned, despairing. "It'll never get to him on time! Even if a messenger left right now on a horse for London Town, he might not find him. I'll have to go myself."

Denzil grabbed his cloak, threw it around his shoulders, and ran to the door. It was black as a witch's cauldron outside. He had no idea which direction to go. He'd never been more than three days' journey outside his village. Even if he turned himself into a hare and ran like the wind, he might never find London Town, let alone Valvasor. And there were robbers out in the dark world, and highwaymen, and wolves.

He came back inside and bolted the door, then went and stood by the table, staring at the books of spells, thinking. He was panting from fear, and shaking all over. He needed Valvasor. He couldn't live if Valvasor was dead. He'd starve. Besides, the master hadn't taught him all the magic yet.

Magic!

"I'll warn him with magic!" he yelled, pulling a candle closer to the old books on the table. Frantically, he turned the pages. "Spell to make a fish take the hook," he read. "No. Useless, that. Can't cook them when I do catch them.

Spell to make a maiden fall in love. Soppy stuff. They'd be better off falling in a lake. What's this? Spell to travel to next week. No. That's no use. It has to be Wednesday. Spy Wednesday." He read for a while longer, turning the pages with trembling hands. "Here it is!" he cried, suddenly. "Spell to go to Wednesday. That's it! I'll go to Spy Wednesday in London Town, and warn him!"

He read through the spell carefully, his shaking fingers underlining the words. It was a long spell containing many calculations and numbers. He had to work out numbers of hours and days, the number of miles to London Town, the positions of the stars, and the exact time the sun was in its zenith, whatever that was. He leaned his head in his hands, bewildered. So many calculations! He was good at sums, but not that good. Yet it had to be done. And he was the one to do it. He pulled over a high stool to sit on, dragged the big book closer, picked up a dripping candle, and leaned over the page.

All night he studied the spell, making notes and long trailing sums in the margins, getting ink all over his fingers and on his shirt. He muttered and swore, looked things up in other books, went out and looked at the stars, muttered and swore again, and did some more sums. But by morning he'd worked it out. He was sure he had. He hoped he had.

He checked his calculations one last time, and wrote the results into the correct spaces in the magic chant. He whispered the whole thing through twenty times until he could say every word without making a mistake. Then he went to the bearskin on the floor, reached between the teeth of the great stuffed head, and drew out a key. He went over to one of the cupboards and unlocked it.

All Valvasor's most powerful magic things were here. Mighty charms, magic runes carved into polished bones, small goblin shoes, finger-bones from saints and queens, magic stones and necklaces, a knife used by the great Merlin long ago . . . and a thousand other things, all secret and sacred and immensely powerful.

Denzil stood staring at them, his heart thundering. He dared not touch anything save that one thing he looked for. He saw it at last, hanging on a leather thong from a bone hook. Reaching over, Denzil took it down, careful to touch nothing else. He turned it over and over in his hands, hearing his heart drumming in his ears, feeling his throat throbbing and dry. In his hands, he held the most powerful thing in all the world to do with Time.

It was a flat medallion about the size of a large coin. On one side it was silver, like the full moon. The other side was gold, and symbolized the sun. There was a tiny catch on one side, so small you had to look carefully to find it. Denzil pressed the catch with the edge of his thumbnail, and the silver and gold halves flew open. Curled round inside the silver moon was a lock of pure white hair.

"Noah's beard," breathed Denzil, stroking it

gently with a tip of one finger. "Taken from him when he was nearly a thousand years old."

Carefully he closed the silver and gold halves, and hung the charm around his neck. He closed and locked the cupboard, and returned the key to its hiding place.

Back with the book of spells, Denzil copied out the magic chant with great care. It was too long to remember, but it would still work if he read it aloud – so long as he read it without making a single mistake. If he messed up even one word, it would change everything.

He checked it through, then went outside and faced the rising sun. It was a beautiful morning. The village cottages were veiled in mist, and the fields all around were pink in the early light. The sun shimmered like melting gold on the horizon, and glinted on the holy charm that lay on Denzil's chest.

Denzil lifted the written spell high, and wished the paper didn't shake so much. He was terrified of what he was doing, and terrified of what would happen if it wasn't done. For Valvasor, he thought desperately. And for me. So he can come back and teach all the rest to me.

He took a deep breath, held up the paper in both hands, and spoke the magic chant.

Time of tomorrow,
hours of today,
endless and trackless
and timeless the day;
upstream or downstream,
nine through to nil,
shoreless and moonless,
sunless and still,
give me tomorrow,
lend me today,
I want to borrow
time yesterday.

Fly the full circle,
beginning and end,
endless and trackless,

no time to spend;
past time and lifetime
are all clockwork lies –
anytime, sometime,
timeless it flies!
Fly to five thousand,
onward to dawn!
Yesterday's coming,
tomorrow I'm born.

Life is eternal,
ten thousand and six,
straight to the centre
and all time is nix!
Anytime, sometime,
and meantime I choose
fast forward to Wednesday,
no time to lose!
Give me Spy Wednesday,
lend me somehow
time in Spy Wednesday,
anytime – NOW!

Wave after wave of rainbow light poured over him. The colours deepened, rang with music and laughter, and from somewhere far away he heard children singing, young people talking, and old people whispering. Still the light poured over him. He seemed drenched in it, and there was no village around him, no grass beneath him, no familiar earth, nothing. Just light, throbbing and alive and brilliant with colour. Numbers flashed in front of him; numbers from the pages of calendars, the names of days, and the numbers of years. The numbers surrounded him, swept him up until he flew in them, flew through vast distances, with a huge wind rushing all around.

Suddenly, all was still. The light, the colours, the numbers, the rushing wind – all were gone. He was standing in darkness, still holding the paper in front of his face.

Slowly he lowered it and looked around.

Chapter 3

Meeting Sam

It was night. There were strange sounds all round; music, sharp and thumping, and drums. A man was singing, but it sounded as if he was suffering horribly. Denzil could hear people talking, but their voices sounded hollow and strange, as if they were speaking down a well. Somewhere a dog barked and a cat yowled. From far in the distance came a weird whooshing sound, and a blaring noise Denzil had never heard before. There were lights glimmering through a few trees, but not flaming lights like fire. The night was full of dark shapes, huge and unknown.

Denzil felt damp and cold, and he looked down at his feet. The grass was all short and even, as if someone had cut it all off. He moved his feet on it, amazed. Whoever would bother to cut grass this neatly? Looking up, he saw nearby a strange thin pole made of metal. It was slightly taller than Denzil, and on the top of it, twirling slowly around like a horizontal spider's web, were thin, shining strings. Clothes hung on the strings – weird clothes. But he knew what they were because he recognized two shirts and a woman's skirt. Most of the other garments were very small and baffled him.

He put the spell on the ground, walked over and touched one of the smaller pieces of clothing. It came off the metal string and he turned the garment over in his hands, marvelling at it. Three holes were in the thing, one large and two small. The material stretched easily, and sprang back into shape again. It must be a hat, he decided. It's the right size. These two small holes must be for your eyes. He pulled the garment over his head, adjusting the holes so he could see through them, and looked around.

Across the flat grass was a building, huge compared with the tiny cottages he was used to. It was all straight lines and strange angles, and had perfectly oblong windows with no shutters. It was different from every building Denzil had ever heard of, or seen. There was no thatch hanging over the edge of the roof, no smoke rising from a cooking-fire inside, and the light behind the windows was different from candle-light – steadier, and bright.

Suddenly there was a noise, and a door in the building flew open. Light flooded across the grass – not soft firelight, but a harsh, brilliant light such as he had never seen before at night.

"Saints alive!" he screamed. "You've got the sun in there!"

Someone came out of the house. He couldn't see the person at first, because the harsh light still blinded him.

"What are you doing here?" asked a voice,

sharply. "Why have you got Theresa's knickers on your head?"

"Theresa's?" he gasped, whipping the thing off. "The *saint's?*" Then he gave a terrible howl, and flung himself on the ground. "Jesus have mercy!" he wailed. "God have mercy! I'm dead! I'm dead!"

A foot kicked his elbow, not gently. He glanced at it sideways, his mouth full of grass, and noticed that the foot wore a pure white shoe, beautifully woven and laced. He'd give anything for a shoe like that. He looked up past the ankle, up the leg covered with lovely blue material, up past a white shirt to a face framed in curls of pure gold. It was a girl. Wearing trousers.

I thought they all wore white nightshirts here, he thought dreamily. And I thought they had wings. Maybe hers are folded up, and I can't see them. Heavens but she's a pretty one.

He bent his head reverently, and kissed the ground near her shoe. "Have mercy, sweet angel," he said. "I'm sorry I pulled the legs off that frog, but I had to, for a spell. I'm sorry I stole the custard tarts, and I didn't mean to look in Mistress Millin's window and see her kiss the baker. I'm sorry I'm a burglar. I'm sorry—"

"Stop whinging and stand up," the girl said.

Shaking like a leaf, he stood. He was the same height as her and looked straight into her face. He couldn't see much detail because the light was behind her, but her hair made a golden halo all around her head, just like the painted angels in church.

"What are you doing here?" she asked.

There was something high and hard about her voice, as if she were an important person here and he was an intruder. He peered at her shadowed face and saw that her mouth was angry and stern. Her eyes glinted like cold blue stone. "What are you doing here?" she asked again, impatiently.

"I don't know," he said, hoarsely. "I honestly thought I'd got to the other place. You won't send me there, will you? Not now. Not now that I'm here. I promise I'll be good. I promise with all my heart." He wrung his hands, pleadingly.

She almost smiled, and shook her head in bewilderment. Blimey, he was dirty. And he smelt like fish and smoke and old socks. His hair looked as if it hadn't been washed for years. She noticed a beautiful gold medallion around his neck, and wondered if he'd stolen it.

"I'm taking you to my father," she said. "He'll call the police. You shouldn't pinch clothes from people's clotheslines. Especially knickers. It's not nice."

Denzil hung his head, and tears poured down his cheeks. "Not the Father, please," he begged. "Take me to Mother Mary, or Saint Peter."

"Saint Peter!" She burst out laughing, and he lifted his head, his nostrils flaring, green eyes on fire.

"Don't laugh!" he shouted. "It's all right for

you. You're already an angel. I'm only a wizard. You could show a bit of pity."

"A wizard?" she asked, still laughing.

"Yes! And I'm a good one."

"What's your name?"

Denzil drew himself up to his full height, puffed out his chest, and announced proudly: "Denzil. I'm wizard apprentice to the great Valvasor."

"Is that so?" she said, smiling. "I'm Sam."

"Sam? Are you a boy after all?" He sounded disappointed.

"No. My real name's Samantha, but everyone calls me Sam."

"And you all wear trousers here? And you fly?"

"Only when I've got wings on," she said, laughing again. "I have to watch out for tall trees though, and aeroplanes and things."

"I fly, too," he said excitedly. "I got tangled up with a kite, once. But I've never seen a—a—erraplane?"

"You must fly with your eyes shut then," she said.

"I do not! I have excellent eyesight when I'm flying! I like being a falcon best, they're so fast. I was a sparrow once, but the miller's cat nearly got me."

Curious, Sam looked him up and down, closely. "You do look a bit like a sparrow," she said. "A lot more like a sparrow than a wizard."

Denzil stuck his chin out, and for a moment she thought he was going to hit her. She clenched her fists, ready.

"I'm a good wizard!" he hissed. "Almost as good as Valvasor!"

"Prove it then," she said.

He held out his hand, and she saw that it was empty, dirty, and smudged with black dye of some sort. He closed his hand, breathed a few words she didn't understand, and opened his fingers. On his palm was an egg, smooth and shining.

"That's not magic," she said. "That was

hidden up your sleeve. My father can do that."

The egg cracked open, and a tiny chick wobbled out. It sat there opening and shutting its beak, cheeping pitifully.

"Not bad," she murmured, slightly impressed. "Your timing's terrific. But you're cruel. The poor thing needs its mother."

While she watched, the chick grew. Quickly – so quickly that Sam didn't dare blink in case she missed something – it grew feathers, puffed up to the size of a thrush and then to the size of a seagull, and still it grew. It was sleek and shining and pure black, with a curving beak and slanting, cunning eyes. She backed away, opening her mouth to speak, but no words came.

"It's a falcon," said Denzil proudly. He tilted his arm, and the bird clambered up onto his wrist. Its claws dug into his flesh but he didn't seem to mind. Suddenly he lifted his arm, flinging the bird high into the air. It flew away, shrieking a strange, wild cry, and they saw it wheeling against the moon.

Denzil looked at the girl, and saw that she had turned pale. He smiled, satisfied. "I told you I was good," he said. "Do you want to see some more?"

She shook her head. "No . . . not right now," she said, in a small voice. "Where are you from, Denzil? What year?"

"1291," he replied. "I suppose you don't have years, in heaven. Here it's for ever and ever, isn't it?"

"You're not in heaven," she said, starting to smile again. "Nowhere near it."

"I'm still alive then?" he cried. "Is it Wednesday?"

"Yes."

He sighed, relieved. "That's all right then. I was aiming for Spy Wednesday. Is this London Town?"

"No. It's Londfield. And it's 1991. You've skipped a few centuries, haven't you?"

His face went grey. "Gawd," he said. "Seven. I've skipped seven hundred years."

"How many did you want to miss?"

"Four days," he replied, chewing his lower lip. "I've made a little mistake somewhere."

"Samantha!" called someone, from the door behind them. Sam looked around, startled. A woman stood in the bright doorway, holding a cloth. "It's your turn to dry the dishes," she called. "Who's your friend?"

"Denzil," Sam called back, trying to hide him with her shadow. He was wearing a short shirt, tights with holes in them, and no trousers at all. Her mum would have a fit if she saw him.

"You're new around here, are you, Denzil?" asked Sam's mother, peering at him through the darkness.

"He just dropped in," said Sam. "He's going now."

"Tell him he can come back tomorrow and see you," said her mother, as she went back inside.

"You'd better go," said Sam. "Will I see you again?"

"I don't know," he muttered, and suddenly gripped her arm. "This is Spy Wednesday, isn't it?"

"I don't know. I think it's just Wednesday." She sniffed, and wrinkled her nose. "When was your last bath, Denzil?"

"Christmas," he said, then groaned and covered his face with his hands.

"It doesn't matter," she said softly. "You can have a bath at our place. Mum won't mind."

"It's not that," he said. "That can wait till next Christmas. But I need Spy Wednesday. I've got it all wrong."

"You've got the right day," she reminded him gently. "It is Wednesday. You were pretty clever to get that right. It's not your fault if it's the wrong Wednesday."

"You don't understand!" he cried in desperation. "I've got to go to London on Spy Wednesday! I have to! I'll have to work on my sums again, and get the year right, as well. That should help." He looked calmer, and very determined. He bent and picked up a sheet of paper off the grass. "I'll see you tomorrow then," he said.

"Where will you sleep?"

He shrugged. "I'm not fussy. Under a hedge somewhere."

"Samantha!" called her mother from the house. "Come in right now and do the dishes!"

"Have to go," she said. "Don't sleep under a hedge, Denzil. There's a treehouse up there, in that big pine at the bottom of our place. There's a blanket, some cushions, and a packet of chocolate biscuits behind the books. But don't let Murgatroyd out – you'll never catch him again."

She raced inside, the door banged shut, and she was gone.

"Who's Murgatroyd?" Denzil called after her.

But she didn't come out again and, after a time, he turned and walked down the sloping grass to the dark, whispering pine.

Chapter 4

Denzil Gets His Orders

S am gulped down her muesli, and watched anxiously while her mother made her school lunch.

"Can I have four extra sandwiches, today, please Mum?" Sam asked, with her mouth full. "And two more muffins, and another apple?"

Mrs MacAllister glanced over her shoulder, surprised. "Planning to have a hungry day?" she asked.

Sam nodded. "I'll be starving all day," she said. "You'd better make that three extra muffins. Thanks, Mum."

Sam's older brother, Travis, leaned across the table and winked at her. "Got a hungry friend?" he whispered, and she nodded.

Sam loved Travis: he was seventeen and rode a motorbike. He took her on it sometimes, but they never told their mother.

"A furry friend?" prompted Travis. "Another stray?"

"No." Sam glanced at her ginger cat, Joplin, crouched greedily over his breakfast on the kitchen floor. "A stray," she whispered, "but not a furry one. Not *very* furry, anyway. He's a boy."

"A *human?*" spluttered Travis, spraying marmalade everywhere.

Mrs MacAllister turned around and placed Sam's school lunch on the table. "What's human?" she asked.

"Inhuman," said Travis quickly. "Sam's appetite. It's inhuman. She should have been a dragon, and we could feed her all the scraps, stoke her up with coal, and rent her out as a barbecue lighter."

"That's not nice," murmured his mother.

"I think it is," said Sam. "I like dragons." She got up, collected her school lunch, and disappeared into her room to share out some of the lunch for Denzil. Her sister, Theresa, was in there looking for something.

Theresa was sixteen, tall and slim, with big blue eyes and curving lips. Travis's friends came around at the weekends, supposedly to see Travis, but they usually ended up hanging around Theresa. Sam couldn't understand why. She thought Theresa was sulky and bad-tempered; and anyway, she already had a boyfriend. Right now no one would want to see her: she had no makeup on and her glossy, bronze curls were straggly and dark and dripping all over her college uniform. Theresa didn't look pleased.

"What have you done with my hairdryer?" she asked.

"It's in the laundry," replied Sam, unwrapping her lunch. She was disappointed. Her mother had made only one extra sandwich, and given her one more apple. There were no extra muffins.

Theresa stood facing her, hands on hips, two spots of angry red in her cheeks. "And what's my hairdryer doing out there?" she demanded. "I suppose you dried your cat with it the last time you shampooed him. It's not right to bathe a cat, you know. They wash themselves."

She stormed out, and Sam yelled after her: "He can't lick off lipstick!"

Theresa came marching back, furious. "My lipstick, I suppose?" she cried. "I didn't say you could use my things. And what was it doing on the cat?"

"Making him pink," said Sam. "I was turning him into the pink panther."

Theresa's face went a motley shade of purple. "That was my brand-new lipstick! Give it back!"

"I can't," said Sam calmly, dividing her lunch roughly in half. "It's full of Joplin's fur, and he's eaten most of it. I gave the rest of it to Murgatroyd to play with. He likes shiny things."

"You gave it to your rat?" shrieked Theresa. "That's it, Samantha! The next time you go into my room and touch my things, I'm going to rip the hair off your doll."

"I don't care," said Sam, putting Denzil's share of the lunch in a paper bag.

"I'll tear up that cardboard circus Grandma gave you!" hissed Theresa.

"I don't care," said Sam.

"I'll go and wreck your treehouse."

Sam's head jerked up, and her blue eyes glittered. Theresa smiled a triumphant little smile, and went out.

Muttering, Sam picked up Denzil's lunch and went outside to the treehouse. Joplin trotted after her, hoping for another chance to nab Murgatroyd.

"You stay here," commanded Sam, holding the bag of sandwiches in her teeth, so she could climb the ladder. "You're in enough trouble already."

She clambered off the top of the ladder, and stood for a few minutes on the platform outside the treehouse door, listening. It was deadly quiet inside. Noiselessly, she opened the door and went in.

The place was a shambles. All her precious books were lying on the floor, and some of the pages had been torn out. The loose pages, covered with numbers written in red crayon, were all over the floor, mingled with pieces of Lego. One of the cushions had a large hole burnt in it, and the cloudy stuffing was all over the place. There was a small mattress taking up most of the floor, which was where Sam sometimes slept; but no one was sleeping there now. And Murgatroyd's cage was wide open.

"Denzil!" roared Sam. "Where are you?"

She stamped her foot, and a chocolate biscuit stuck to the bottom of her sandal. She sat on the mattress and picked the biscuit off, throwing it out the open door. Looking around, she almost cried. Her precious treehouse, ruined. It'd take her hours and hours to clean it up. She wished she didn't have to go to school.

"Denzil?" she called out again, softly this time. Maybe he was hiding because he was scared. But where? The place was so small, there was nowhere he could hide. A terrible thought struck her. Maybe he had run away, and taken Murgatroyd with him.

She rushed out to the small platform, and peered out across the newly-mown lawn and down the drive to the road. There was a quiet movement behind her, and she spun around. Denzil was sitting on the exploded cushion, stroking Murgatroyd.

For a whole minute Sam stared at him, speechless, her face white. She didn't ask how he'd got in, but she had creepy shivers up and down her spine, and she felt suddenly cold and afraid. Slowly, she took Murgatroyd out of Denzil's hands, and put the rat back in his cage.

Then she faced Denzil again. He was staring hard at her face and she felt uncomfortable.

She didn't look like any other girl he knew. All the girls in Denzil's village were cringing, timid things. He never knew whether that was the way girls were, or whether they were only like that with him, because he was a wizard. But this girl was different. She was scared of him too, right now, but she still looked him straight in the eye and was still cool and queenly. She had eyes the colour of a robin's eggs, and long lashes the colour of honey. Her brows were straight, almost hidden under her long, blonde curls, and her mouth was a mixture of toughness, fear and friendliness. There was something honest and brave about her. He guessed, correctly, that she was about twelve – just a year older than himself.

His thoughtful stare gave Sam time to gather her wits. She decided to forget he was a wizard and tried to sound angry.

"Where have you been?" she asked irritably.

"I've been here all the time," he replied. He was almost tempted to turn his head into a lion's just to show her who was the boss, but he changed his mind. "I was in the cushion," he added. "Curled up asleep with Murgatroyd."

Sam opened her mouth to speak, but nothing came out. Denzil's mouth twitched in an odd little smile, and he said: "He got out of his cage. I couldn't catch him, so I turned myself into a rat and made friends with him. We had lots of fun. The tarts were lovely."

"Tarts?" croaked Sam, sitting down.

Denzil pointed to a smudge of chocolate near her foot. "Those tarts," he said.

Sam took a deep breath, and frowned. "I told you not to let him out of his cage," she said. "And look what you've done to my books."

"I was doing my sums again," he explained. "Working out how to find Spy Wednesday. I wrote down all the calculations while I could remember them. If I forget those, I'm stuck here for good."

Sam couldn't think of anything worse. She pointed to the scorched cushion. "How did that get burnt?" she demanded.

"I made a candle so I could see to do the sums and things. The pillow caught fire."

Sam stood up and handed him the bag of sandwiches. She wished now she'd kept the peanut butter and jam one for herself. "This is your lunch," she said. "When I get home I want to find this whole place cleaned up. And the cushion fixed. You can make yourself a needle and cotton, and sew it up."

"Sew?" he cried, horrified. "Sew? Me do sewing?"

"And cleaning up," she said.

Denzil stuck his chin out, and his green eyes flashed. "Never! Never in a hundred years! It's woman's work!"

Sam grabbed him by the shirt, and dragged him so close that their noses almost touched. "If I ever hear you say that again," she said, "I'll punch your lights out. You'll tidy all this up, *and* you'll sew up the cushion, *and* you'll mend the books. And when I come in after school, I expect a bottle of lemonade and an ice-cream. Strawberry flavoured. If you can turn yourself into a rat, making ice-cream should be easy."

"Strawberries?" he choked.

"Yes. With chocolate chips." She let him go, and he fell against the wall. "And when you've done all that," she said as she went out, "you can have a wash. You smell worse than Murgatroyd."

She shut the door behind her, and Denzil stuck out his tongue. He waited until he heard her jump off the end of the ladder, then he took Murgatroyd out of his cage again. He sat in the middle of the messy treehouse, rocking Murgatroyd and stroking his long white tail.

"We won't do it, will we?" he murmured. "We'll work out our sums and get the answers right, and when Sammy Snarlybritches comes back, we'll be gone. Both of us."

With Murgatroyd curled about his neck, he knelt down, picked up a purple crayon, and tore another page out of a book.

Chapter 5

Denzil in Trouble

Denzil hadn't been doing his sums long, when he heard noises from below. He opened the treehouse door, crept on all fours to the edge of the platform, and peered down.

A man and a woman came out of the house, wearing funny clothes. The man was tall and handsome, with thick, black hair and a fine, scowling face. The woman was almost as tall as he was, with short fair hair and a bright, sunny face. Laughing and chattering, she seemed to be the opposite of the man. She was wearing a white dress so short that Denzil could see her ankles – even some of her leg. He stared, fascinated.

The man kissed the woman, and she went into a small wooden building beside the house. A few moments later, Denzil heard a roar worse than anything in his nightmares, and a bright red shining thing swished out of the building, rumbled out of sight beside the house, and thundered off into the distance.

Denzil gripped the edge of the platform, feeling dizzy and sick. Whatever the thing was, it had eaten the woman. He'd glimpsed the insides of it, and seen her white skirt and legs. He waited, breathless, for the man to rush after it and rescue her. But he didn't. He bent and pulled a weed out of the garden, whistled a little tune, went back into the house and closed the door.

"Coward!" Denzil screamed after him. "Sissy! Chicken-livered milksop! Get your sword and go and save her!"

The man poked his head out the door again,

and looked all around the garden. Fortunately for Denzil, at that moment the platform he was on tilted, and he almost fell off. He scrambled back, and the man didn't see him. When Denzil got his balance and looked over the edge again, the man was gone. But he came out a short while later and went into the same small wooden building.

He soon appeared riding two skinny wheels held together by thin pipes. Denzil cracked up laughing, and nearly fell off his perch again. Luckily the man didn't hear him, but rode off slowly, still whistling, his long, thin legs working round and round in silly little circles. He, too, disappeared around the far side of the house. Denzil rolled on the platform, hooting and clutching his ribs. He hadn't seen anything that funny since Friar Fattyface had sat on a donkey and squashed it.

When he'd stopped laughing, Denzil went back into the treehouse. He picked up Murga-troyd, who was busy gobbling biscuit crumbs, and turned to the pages of sums. He worked hard for a while, writing down numbers and crossing them out again. Suddenly he swore and hurled the crayon across the room. He buried his face in his hands. "I'll never do it," he groaned.

After a while he gave a huge sigh, lifted his head, and took off the magic charm that hung about his neck. He flicked it open and took out the lock of Noah's beard. It lay on his dirty palm, snow white and glowing with holiness and power. Denzil bent his head reverently and kissed the precious hair, then curled it carefully back into the silver disc. He closed the medallion halves, put the charm down on the piece of paper containing the magic spell, and turned back to his sums again.

"I've got to find Spy Wednesday," he muttered, desperately, his face determined and grim. "I've got to warn Valvasor about the dragon. I've got to find him on Spy Wednesday, and save him. Otherwise, he dies."

But after an hour of scribbling and smudging

out and scribbling again, he gave up. He picked up the thing Sam had called his lunch, and sniffed it. It smelled delicious. He opened the bag, and stared in amazement at the pale brown bread, almost as smooth and square as a page of parchment. He took a bite and chewed cautiously. Then he ate faster, cramming the sandwiches into his mouth, moaning with delight. Murgatroyd scrambled up the front of his shirt and tried to eat the crusts dangling from Denzil's mouth, but Denzil knocked him away. Murgatroyd left a few droppings and a wet patch on Denzil's knee, and climbed down to try the muffin.

Five minutes later, still hungry and smelling slightly worse than he had before, Denzil left the treehouse and climbed down the ladder, with Murgatroyd tucked inside his shirt. He went over to the big house and stood outside the door, listening. It was quiet as a grave inside. He lifted his hand and tried the door handle. It was a strange one, and Denzil didn't know whether he was working it properly, or whether the door was locked. He took Murgatroyd out of his shirt and poked him under the gap at the bottom of the door. Then he stood back, made himself very still, and muttered a spell.

Slowly, his face became long and thin. His eyes grew round and very black. Large ears appeared through his thick hair, which now grew rapidly down across his cheeks and along his pointed nose. His clothes vanished. His whole body was covered in fur. His hands shrank to tiny paws, hairless and human-like, but with tiny pink claws. His feet became like back paws, long-toed and clawed. And all the time he became smaller, his whole body drawing in, sinking, shrinking, until all that had been Denzil was just a large brown rat sitting on the step.

He peeped under the door, sniffing, quivering with excitement. He could smell Murgatroyd on the other side, and a thousand other thrilling smells. He squeezed under the door and into the MacAllisters' house.

Still a rat, he stood upright on his back legs like a miniature kangaroo, sniffing hard. There was so much to smell! Strange scented soapy smells, the fragrance of unfamiliar foods, rubber-soled shoes, lino, carpet, plastics, paint – a hundred things he'd never smelled before. He had no idea what the smells were, of course. He knew only that here was a new world, more shining and marvellous than anything he had ever seen.

Quickly, he changed into his own body. It didn't take long to be Denzil again; that part was easy, like slipping into old loved clothes, and was done in a few seconds. He looked around, eyes popping.

Everything in the kitchen shone: the green painted walls, the creamy cupboards and shelves, the incredible clear glass windows, the strange white cabinets with bright metal strips and cold glossy surfaces, the polished floor, the fantastic glittering machines fixed to the walls.

In a daze, Denzil ran his hands over the bright

taps, rubbed the gleaming worktops, the smooth walls, and the amazing windows of glass. Everything was wonderful, weird, and bewildering. He fingered brightly coloured packets in the pantry, crackled the bags of puzzling new foods, scooped up fingerfuls of rich butter, and licked the sticky rims of jars of jam and marmalade. He discovered a strange yellow container of honey, and dug it all out with his fingers, licking them clean and moaning with ecstasy. He munched on macaroni, rolled oats, and long, uncooked spaghetti. Then, satisfied and dripping with honey, jam, and globs of half-chewed muesli, he decided to explore the rest of the house.

Sam ran all the way home after school, threw her schoolbag onto the back doorstep, and raced over to the treehouse. She climbed the ladder quickly, eager for her ice-cream and lemonade. She threw open the treehouse door – then stood there, astounded and furious.

Nothing had been tidied up. In fact the mess

was even worse. And Denzil was lying flat on his back in the middle of it, wearing Travis's purple pyjama jacket, Mrs MacAllister's wedding hat, and Theresa's pink ballet tights. He was snoring his head off.

Sam picked up what was left of the cushion and hit Denzil over the head with it. Stuffing flew everywhere, and Denzil shot up, screaming. "Help!" he cried, half-blinded and choked by fluff and stuffing. "Help! War! Blizzard! Attack!"

"You didn't do what I said!" shouted Sam. "I told you to clean this place up! I told you to make ice-cream and lemonade! And you've been dressing up, instead. Where did you get all that stuff?"

"In the manor hall," he replied, trying to look cool and dignified. He wasn't used to being hit over the head, especially by a girl.

"Where?" cried Sam.

"The manor hall. You know. Down there." He pointed out the treehouse window towards her home.

"You've been in our house?"

"Yes. I had a look around. Found some new clothes."

"How did you get in? It was locked up."

"I turned myself into a rat and crept under the door."

"Take them off."

"What?"

"The clothes. They're not yours."

"They are now. I burglared them."

"Take them off! You look stupid. Mum wore that hat on her wedding day. She'll kill you when she sees it. You've squashed it."

"I didn't squash it. You did, when you clouted me. Anyway, she can't."

"Can't what?"

"Can't kill me. I'll wear a suit of armour, and shoot her with a longbow. Anyway, she's already dead. A beast ate her this morning. Legs and all."

Sam turned white. "What beast?"

"A roaring, shiny one. Red. It was waiting in that building down there, beside the manor hall. Your father just watched, too. Didn't save her or anything. Just watched."

Sam thought, quickly. Then she giggled. "That was the car, stupid."

"Whatever it was, it ate her."

"You've got a lot to learn, Denzil. And you can start by taking those clothes off, and putting them back where they came from."

"I'm not taking these off! I'm not running around naked!"

"Why not? You wouldn't look any sillier than you do now."

Denzil drew himself up to his full height, puffed out his chest, and said haughtily: "These, lady, are the best clothes I've ever had. Even Sir Godric would be proud of these. He had pink hose once, but they weren't as smooth as mine."

"Yours are ballet tights," said Sam, starting to laugh. "And who's Sir Godric?"

"He's the village lord. Owns thirty oxen, he does. And the windmill. And the bakehouse."

"Good for him," said Sam. "Well, I own this

treehouse. And if you don't clean it up right now, I'm throwing you out. And I'll tear up all your sums."

Denzil gulped. "Not my sums," he said huskily. "I've just about got them right."

"Clean up," said Sam.

"I'll do it tomorrow."

"Now," said Sam.

Denzil sighed, rubbed a bump on his head, and started picking up the crayons. Sam sat on the mattress and watched.

It took Denzil an hour to clean it up. He used magic to sew up the cushion and mend the books. Sam suspected that was cheating, but let him get away with it because it was terrific to watch. The pages just grew back again, unrolling like leaves, perfect and whole. Some of the words were jumbled on the new pages, and the pictures looked very strange, but she could put up with that. Finally, he made a tidy pile of his calculations, placed the spell on top – upside-down so no one could read it – and put the gold and silver medallion on top of it all.

"What's that gold thing?" asked Sam, curiously. "Something you stole?"

"It's magic," said Denzil, putting the precious pile carefully into the bookshelf. "I'll leave the charm with the sums, and the magic might go into them and make them right." Suddenly alarmed, he looked back at Sam. "No one will come in here, will they?" he asked. "No one'll touch these things? If anything's lost, I'm stuck here forever."

Sam shook her head. "No one ever comes in here except me. And I won't touch anything. I promise."

Denzil looked relieved. He sat down on the mattress beside Sam, and leaned back on the tidied cushions as if he owned the place.

"It looks pretty fine, now," he commented, surveying the room. "Fit for a king."

"It's not bad," said Sam, standing up. "Make sure it stays like this. You can have a rest now, and later on I'll bring you some dinner."

"A thousand thanks, sweet lady," said Denzil politely.

But after she went out, he stuck out his tongue.

Sam got the house key from its hiding place, and unlocked the back door. No one else was home yet; her mother was at work, her father was probably out looking for another job, and Travis was working at the garage. Theresa would be home from college soon, unless she'd gone to visit her boyfriend.

Sam went inside, and straight to the pantry to find something to eat. Her feet made crunchy noises on the floor. Rice and rolled oats were everywhere. All the packets on the shelves had been opened, and the shelves were littered with food. It looked as if someone had sneezed into the packet of cocoa, and the whole pantry was powdered in a fine layer of brown. Sam picked up the biscuit tin. At least he hadn't figured out how to open that. She took out a handful of gingernuts, and wandered into her bedroom.

Someone had been bouncing on her bed. And they'd been licking the mirror, smudging jam and honey all over it. Her wardrobe door was open, and half her clothes had been pulled off the hangers and dropped on the floor. She sighed, then laughed quietly, lay down on her bed and ate another gingernut. She heard Theresa arrive home from college. She heard her put on the kettle for a cup of coffee, then come up the passage to her room. It was next to Sam's, and as she went past Theresa called, "Hi, Sis."

"Hi," replied Sam with her mouth full. She heard Theresa drop her schoolbag on the floor, and for a while there was silence. Usually Theresa turned on her radio straight away. Today she didn't. She came back to Sam's room and stood leaning in the doorway, a strange expression on her face.

"Had a good day?" Theresa asked. She wasn't smiling.

"Okay," said Sam. "Simon Turrin was sick

today all over his desk. Do you want a ginger-nut?"

Theresa didn't answer. She returned to the kitchen, turned off the boiling kettle, and went outside.

Sam finished the gingernuts, and went into the lounge to watch television. After a while she heard her father come home, and not long after that Travis's motorbike roared up the drive. Sam went out to the kitchen and opened the pantry door.

"Oh, no, you don't," said her father, putting a saucepan of carrots on the stove. "You won't eat your dinner. By the look of the pantry you've already been in there helping yourself. You can go next door and borrow an egg for me. I need one for the dessert. And when you get back, you can clean up that pantry."

"What is dessert?" asked Sam.

"Custard," her father answered and she pulled a face.

Once outside, she noticed that the house

across the road was no longer empty. The big FOR SALE sign had been taken down, and there was a black bird in a red cage hanging in the veranda. The house windows were all open, and pot plants had been put on the windowsills and on the front steps. A pitch-black cat sat on the steps, staring across at Sam with blazing yellow eyes. Suddenly she realized it wasn't watching her at all, but Joplin, who had paused by the postbox, back arched, his tail frizzy with fury. For six months that empty property had been Joplin's hunting ground, and he wasn't going to give it up without a fight.

"No you don't!" cried Sam, but it was too late. Without stopping to look for traffic, Joplin was across the road, up the steps, and at war with the black cat. It was a terrific fight. By the time Sam got there, the new cat had taken off across five gardens, and had vanished in the supermarket carpark. The veranda steps were covered with ginger and black fur.

"You shouldn't have done that," murmured

Sam, smoothing Joplin's ruffled ginger fur, and noticing that both his ears were torn. "You don't own this place any more. You'll have to go and bother the mice somewhere else."

Joplin licked his war wounds, his eyes half closed with secret satisfaction. The door behind them opened, and Sam jumped, ready to grab Joplin and run. In the doorway stood an old woman, thin and bent, with hair like a bird's nest and a face like a cheerful chicken.

"Hello, dearie," the old woman croaked. "I thought I heard something." She caught sight of Joplin and clucked in dismay. "Heavens – whatever happened to my cat? He was black half an hour ago."

"This one's mine," said Sam, smiling. "They fought. Yours ran away."

The woman hobbled out onto the veranda, and peered closely at Joplin. Sam studied the old woman. She seemed different from other people Sam knew. She was older than Sam's grandmother, older even than Mr Cavendish who lived down the road and who was a hundred and two; older than anyone, and very mysterious. She had a strange smell about her, like plants, that Sam liked.

The old woman noticed Sam watching her and she chuckled softly. "I'm Mrs Utherwise, dearie," she said. "I've come here to live for a little while."

"I'm Sam. Sam MacAllister, from that green house across the road. I'm supposed to be borrowing an egg from someone. Have you got one I can have?"

"Sam," murmured Mrs Utherwise, thoughtfully. She looked across the road at Sam's house, her eyes screwed almost shut, as if she were trying to see through the walls. "Is there anyone else at your house?" she asked.

"My brother Travis, and my sister Theresa. And Mum and Dad."

"No one else?"

"No."

"Are you sure?" asked Mrs Utherwise, looking worried.

"I've got a rat called Murgatroyd," Sam said helpfully.

"Anyone else?" muttered the old woman. "Oh dear. Are you quite sure?"

"Well . . . there's Denzil," said Sam, hesitantly. "He's only staying for a while. But don't say anything to Mum and Dad. They don't know. Mrs Utherwise? Do you think you could lend me an egg, please? Dad's waiting."

Mrs Utherwise was smiling quietly to herself, and didn't answer.

"Please?" said Sam, more loudly. "An egg. May I borrow one?"

Mrs Utherwise nodded suddenly, and went back inside. She returned with a small pottery jar labelled "Nutmeg".

"Not nutmeg," said Sam. "An egg. You know – oval, and white. An egg."

Mrs Utherwise shuffled back inside again, and came out with the biggest egg Sam had ever seen. Sam took it and examined it carefully. "It's big, isn't it?" she said. "And it's a funny colour. It's not rotten, is it?"

"It's a goose egg, dearie," said Mrs Utherwise. "And don't borrow it. Keep it. I don't want it back."

Sam grinned. "Thanks," she said, and headed home. As she walked back up her driveway, she noticed a movement beside the house. She stopped. It was a sparrow, rather pale and scruffy-looking, hopping along close beside the wall. Quickly, Sam looked around for Joplin. He was over on Mrs Utherwise's steps, pretending he still owned them. She looked back at the sparrow, and jumped.

Denzil stood there, looking ruffled and upset. He was still wearing Travis's pyjama jacket and Theresa's tights, though the wedding hat was gone.

"I didn't do it, Sam," he said. "Honest. Cross-my-heart-and-hope-to-die. I didn't do it."

"Do what?" she asked, alarmed.

He glanced behind him, then shook his head. "What have you done, Denzil?" she cried.

"Nothing!" he wailed.

"What?"

He wrung his hands, pleadingly. "Your tree-house," he said. "I didn't mess it up again. Honest."

Sam put the egg on the edge of the drive, and raced around the house to the treehouse. Denzil tore after her, bleating something about innocence and mercy. Travis was working on his motorbike, and he looked up to see what all the noise was about. He glimpsed a scruffy boy in pyjamas and pink ballet tights, and roared with laughter. Then he stopped. "Hey – that's my pyjama jacket!" he yelled. "Come back!" But Denzil was already halfway up the ladder to the treehouse, clutching frantically at Sam's ankles as she went ahead.

"I didn't do it!" he kept saying. "I didn't! Honest!"

The treehouse was a shambles. It was even

worse than it had been before. The curtains had been torn off the windows, and there were crayon marks all over the painted walls. Sam read the words scrawled across the walls in red, angry crayon: "Stay in your own room! Don't touch my things again!"

"A girl did it," said Denzil, anxiously, watching Sam's face. "A big girl, with hair like yours, only darker. She came in like thunder, all muttering and grim and ready to do murder. I flew off, fast. She did all this, then went back into the manor hall."

"Theresa," spat Sam, furious. "It was Theresa." She went back down the ladder, and Denzil peered after her. A young man was standing at the foot of the ladder, looking up at Denzil and laughing.

Denzil went inside, bewildered and frightened.

"They're all mad here!" he groaned, staring at the wrecked treehouse. "Mad! I'd be safer being a mole, and living underground." And slowly, his skin became velvety and dark, his eyes black like tiny beads, his arms short and strong and tipped with claws for burrowing.

Sam jumped off the bottom of the ladder and began to run past Travis, but he grabbed her arm. "Who's the clown up there?" he asked, still chuckling.

Sam pulled free. "Denzil," she said. "He's not a clown, he's a wizard." She ran into the house, shouting for Theresa. Travis scratched his head, smiled to himself, and went back to his motorbike.

Chapter 6

Suspicions

When Mrs MacAllister got home that night, the house was in an uproar. Sam and Theresa were in the middle of the kitchen screaming at each other, Mr MacAllister was burning the dinner and yelling something about needing an egg, Travis was vacuuming the pantry, and a strange-looking animal was digging holes all over the back lawn.

Mrs MacAllister turned off the vacuum cleaner, rescued the dinner, kissed Mr MacAllister to keep him quiet, and calmly told Sam and Theresa that if they said another word they'd be grounded for a week.

"It's not fair!" wailed Sam, stamping off outside.

"A week!" called Mrs MacAllister, cheerfully.

"She started it!" cried Theresa.

"A week for you, too," said Mrs MacAllister.

Theresa bit her tongue and stamped off to tidy up her room.

Travis put the vacuum cleaner away and went up to Sam's treehouse to check out the wizard in the pink tights. There was no one there. The place was a terrible mess, and Travis spent twenty minutes cleaning it up before he went back inside.

Sam sat on the steps of the front porch, her chin in her hands, trying to decide what to do. Joplin came out and wound himself gracefully around her legs, purring and warm. He had golden yolk all over his paws. Sam sighed, remembering the abandoned egg. She couldn't do anything right these days. And it was all Denzil's fault. She sighed again, and looked across the road at Mrs Utherwise's house.

The old lady was on the veranda, feeding something to the bird. Her black cat was by her feet. Sam waved, and Mrs Utherwise waved back.

Travis came out of the door behind Sam, and sat beside her on the step. He handed her a glass of orange juice.

"I thought you might need this," he said. "All that yelling at Theresa must have made your throat sore. What was it all about?"

"She messed up the treehouse," said Sam, sipping the juice.

"Did she? And what did you do to deserve that?"

"She says I went into her room and got into her make-up and tried on all her clothes."

"And did you?"

"No."

"Who did then?"

Sam said nothing.

Travis looked up and down the road, as if searching for someone. "Who were you waving to when I came out?" he asked. "Denzil? Was he back again?"

"No. He's still in my treehouse," she said. "I was waving to Mrs Utherwise over there." She glanced across the road, but Mrs Utherwise had gone back inside. The cat had gone with her. The red cage swung slightly as the bird moved in it, and glinted in the late afternoon light.

"There's no one over there," said Travis. "The place is empty. It's still for sale."

"She moved in today," said Sam. "She's got a black cat with yellow eyes. And a bird, in that cage there."

"What cage?" asked Travis, staring hard at the house, his brown eyes narrowed.

"On the veranda," said Sam.

Travis frowned, puzzled, and Sam laughed. "You're half blind," she giggled. "It's in that red cage there, hanging up."

Travis shook his head, and she grinned and gave him a sip of the orange juice. Travis was always having her on. That was what she loved best about him: he always made her laugh. She looked at him sideways, and thought what a terrific brother he was. He was tall and good-looking, and strong in a gentle kind of way.

He wasn't like Dad, who was always yelling and getting excited. Travis thought about things, but if he got excited about them sometimes, he didn't show it. He said that one performer in the family was enough. The performer was Dad. He'd been an actor, but was a waiter instead now because the theatre he worked at had closed down. Sam didn't understand about money and funding and unemployment, but she knew it made her father sad not to be an actor any more, and she understood when he had to burst out and rant and rave about things, even if he wasn't on stage and getting paid for it. She knew he hated his job at the restaurant because he had to keep quiet and behave himself.

Mum said Sam was like Dad, always yelling and being dramatic. Sam thought she'd rather be like Travis, though – cool and clever and peaceful to be with. Maybe if she was like Travis she wouldn't get angry and yell at Denzil. It wasn't his fault if he didn't know about things. She probably wouldn't manage very well if she went to his place, either. She sighed, feeling guilty, and Travis gave her a quiet smile.

"Thinking about Denzil?"

Sam nodded, but didn't say anything.

"He's not in your treehouse now, you know," he said. "I went in to talk to him, and there was no one there."

"I don't know where he is then," murmured Sam.

"A sneaky little rascal, isn't he?" grinned Travis. "He gets all over the place. It could have been him in Theresa's room, for all we know. And in my room too, and into my pyjamas. He's probably wearing my underpants, as well!"

Sam looked worried, and Travis put his arm around her. "He's probably a very nice stray, but you can't keep him. He must have run away from home. His parents are probably worried sick about him. They've probably got the police out looking for him."

"I told you, he's a wizard," explained Sam, patiently. "He hasn't got a home. Not here, anyway. He's from hundreds of years ago. He's good at turning himself into animals, like birds and rats and things. But he's not very good at maths. That's how he ended up here – he got his calculations wrong. He can't go back until he's got them right and found out when Spy Wednesday is. He wants to warn his master about a dragon."

Travis thought about that for a while. Then he said, as seriously as he could: "Maybe I can help him, Sam. I wasn't too bad at maths when I was at school."

"Will you?" Sam's face was bright with excitement. "Will you, Travis? But you can't tell Mum and Dad. I'll let you meet Denzil, but they can't. They won't believe he's a wizard.

They'll take him to the police, and he'll have to live in prison or somewhere awful, and he won't be able to do his sums and get back to Spy Wednesday. I want to keep him. For a little while, anyway. He can live in my treehouse. He'll be safe there. Don't tell on him, will you, Travis? Please? Promise?"

Travis sighed, and gave her a grin. "I promise," he said. "After dinner you can let me meet Denzil. That's if he's still around."

Theresa looked up from her dinner and announced that she was going to get a dog.

"What on earth for?" asked Travis.

"You don't have the money for a dog!" said Mr MacAllister. "They're expensive to buy, and they cost a fortune to feed."

"I'm getting a dog," said Theresa firmly. "An Alsatian. A guard dog."

"I think that's silly," said Sam.

"You would!" snapped Theresa. "It'd cramp your style a bit, wouldn't it?"

"What do you mean?" yelled Sam.

"You'd have to stick to your own territory for a change," said Theresa.

"Don't start that all over again," groaned their father.

"A dog's not such a bad idea," murmured Mrs MacAllister. "I've had a feeling lately that someone's been snooping around our place."

There was a sudden silence, and Sam glanced at Travis. He grinned and went on eating his dinner.

"It's just a feeling, really," went on their mother. "I thought I heard someone in our garage last night."

"You should have checked it out," said her husband. "Someone might have been trying to steal the car."

"I looked out the window, but the garage door was still shut," she replied. "And I think someone may have been in our house today. The shoes in my wardrobe were all jumbled up, as if someone had been poking around."

"Someone *was* poking around," said Theresa, stabbing her peas with her fork, and glaring at Sam. "They got into my make-up, too, and tried on my clothes."

Sam said nothing, but her potato stuck in her throat.

"It's not like Sam to do anything like that," murmured Mr MacAllister, thoughtfully, "is it, Sam? And the kitchen was messed up, too, come to think of it. The pantry was an awful mess. Someone had bitten a chunk out of the butter, and the jam jar seemed to have been licked clean around the rim. You kids wouldn't do that."

"Maybe Murgatroyd got inside again," suggested Sam. "He loves butter."

"His tooth marks are different," said Mr MacAllister, remembering. "And something else funny happened this morning. I was just coming back inside when someone yelled out something – something about a coward and a milksop, and a sword."

Mrs MacAllister suddenly put down her knife and fork, and stared hard at Sam. "Sam. Remember that boy you were talking to last night? That new boy in the neighbourhood? What was his name?"

Sam arranged her face to look suitably blank. "Don't remember," she said.

"Yes you do," said her mother. "That skinny boy. Weevil or something. I said he could come back today. After school, I meant. Maybe he's not starting school until next week, and he came back and snooped around here while we were all out."

"If I catch the little beggar, I'll call the police," said Mr MacAllister, looking at his watch. "I'm not having juvenile delinquents hanging around here. Anyway, I've got to run. I'll be late for work. Excuse me, everybody."

He left the table to go and get changed. Sam glanced at Travis again. He smiled and rubbed her ankle with his foot, reassuringly.

"I've got a meeting to go to tonight," said

Mrs MacAllister, also getting up. "It's your turn to do the dishes, Theresa."

"I can't do the dishes," said Theresa. "I'm going out with Adam. He's picking me up in twenty minutes."

"I thought your father told you to finish with him," said her mother. "He's not suitable, Theresa."

"Why not?" asked Theresa, hackles rising. "Isn't he good enough?"

Travis and Sam grinned at each other.

"Just because he's got long hair," went on Theresa hotly. "Just because he wears black leather and doesn't shave. Just because he wears bracelets, and has chains around his neck."

"He ought to have chains around his ankles as well," said her father, coming back into the kitchen. "He looks like he belongs in a dungeon. You're not going out with him, Theresa, and that's that."

"Give me one good reason why," said Theresa, her face red. "First you told me it was because he had a motorbike, and it was dangerous for me to ride pillion. It's okay for Travis to ride one, but not me. So Adam got rid of his motorbike and bought a car, and that's still not good enough. What do you want him to do now – get a glass coach?"

"A rocket would be nice," said her father, putting on his tie, and pulling it so tightly he almost choked himself. "He could go to Mars in that, and we'd be rid of him."

"And I'd go with him!" hissed Theresa. "I hate it here. You're always telling me what to do! I've got no privacy, no say in my own life. I'm sixteen, Dad! I'm old enough to make my own decisions. And I'm definitely old enough to choose my own friends."

Sam got up from the table and put her half-finished dinner on the worktop. Joplin was sitting hopefully by the fridge door, waiting for someone to feed him. She picked him up and took him down to her room, shut the door and sat down on her bed. Joplin sat by the closed door, waiting for it to open and clear the way to the kitchen again. Sam could still hear Theresa shouting. Then her father had his turn. He did the bit about Theresa living under his roof and having to live by his rules. Then Theresa said her piece about leaving school at the end of the year and getting a job and a flat. Sam cheered to herself. She could hardly wait. She'd always wanted Theresa's room.

Joplin started to meow loudly, waiting for someone – anyone – to notice him. Then a flea distracted him, and he put up his hind leg and scratched vigorously behind one ear. There was a strange, wild cry and a thump as something large and invisible crashed into Sam's wardrobe door. Sam shot up, screaming.

Travis rushed in, alarmed.

"There's a thing in my wardrobe!" wailed Sam, flinging her arms around his neck. "An invisible thing!"

Travis glanced over her curly head, and started to laugh. "It's your friend in fancy dress," he said, and Sam turned around.

Denzil stood by the wardrobe, looking battered and dazed. There was a long scratch down his face. He stared at Travis, confused and afraid. Travis grinned at him.

"You get around, don't you, Denzil?" he said. "Sneaking out of wardrobes, now?"

"I wasn't sneaking," said Denzil. "I was on Joplin. He scratched me off."

"I don't blame him," said Travis. "You were probably squashing him."

"He was a flea," explained Sam, sitting down again. "That's how he got in. On Joplin. Why don't you just come in the door, Denzil, like everyone else?"

"Because they'd kick me out," said Denzil, jerking his head towards the kitchen. "I heard what they said. That wild man called me a little beggar. I'm not. I don't beg, I burgle. And I don't hang around. I've never been hung in my life. I've been swung by the feet over the duck pond, and Mistress Armstrong picked me up once and swung me around in her fists, but I've never been hung from a gallows. Never."

Sam giggled, and Travis frowned. He went over to Denzil and studied him hard for a long time. "I don't know where you're from, Denzil," he said. "And I'm not sure I want to know. But I listened to the news before, and no one's reported a missing boy. So I guess as long as no one's looking for you, you can stay here."

Denzil grinned, and hitched up his pink ballet tights. "Thanks," he said. "I just need time to do my sums. Then I'm going to Spy Wednesday, to warn Valvasor. There's a dragon after him."

"Good Lord," murmured Travis.

"The Good Lord won't help him," said Denzil earnestly. "He's not much better at miracles than I am."

A small smile played about Travis's mouth. "You're not modest, that's for sure," he said. Then he leaned forward, and sniffed. "You're not exactly sweet-smelling, either," he added. "When did you last have a bath, Denzil?"

"Christmas," said Denzil.

"Well, it's high time you had another."

"Don't want another."

"If you want to stay with us, you have to. And I'll find you something better to wear than my pyjama jacket and Theresa's ballet tights."

"I thought I looked rather grand," said Denzil, hurt.

"You don't," said Travis. "You look like a girl."

Denzil looked so shocked and insulted that Sam and Travis burst out laughing. Then Travis winked at Sam. "I'll find him some clothes, Sam," he said. "You run him a bath. But make sure the others have left first. We don't want to startle any natives, do we?"

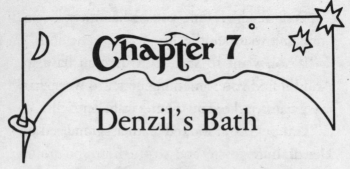

Chapter 7

Denzil's Bath

Sam finished running the bath, checked that it wasn't too hot, and went back to Travis's room. Travis and Denzil were still trying to sort out some clothes for Denzil, not very successfully.

"You can't wear my dressing-gown," Travis was saying for the twentieth time. "I've got some old jeans that are too small for me, and a Harley-Davidson sweatshirt I wore when I was about your age. They'll be a bit big, but they're an improvement on purple pyjamas and pink tights."

"I want this," said Denzil, snatching up the dressing-gown. It was made of black silk, and had blue Chinese dragons embroidered on it.

"You can't wear that," sighed Travis, beginning to lose patience. "You'll look ridiculous."

"No I won't!" cried Denzil, eyes flashing. "Valvasor wears a gown like this! It's his special one! His ceremonial gown! I want one!"

He slipped out of Travis's reach, dragged on the dressing-gown, and strutted around triumphantly. He caught sight of himself in the mirror on Travis's wardrobe door, and stopped, overwhelmed with admiration. "Holy saints!" he murmured. "I look magnificent!" Then he saw Sam watching from the doorway, and bowed grandly.

She clapped and cheered, and he bowed again and gave her a yellow rose.

"Where did it come from?" asked Travis, coming over and inspecting the flower. He sniffed it, and frowned. "It's real!" he muttered. He turned to Denzil, opened the dressing-gown, and checked the pyjama jacket underneath. "Where did you hide the rose, Denzil?" he asked, puzzled.

"I didn't," said Denzil. "I made it. I'm good at flowers. Do you want one?"

"Not as much as you want a bath," said Travis. Denzil pulled a face, and Travis marched him off to the bathroom. Sam followed, giggling.

Denzil saw the bath, and screamed. "I'm not getting into that!" he yelled. "It's boiling!"

Travis leaned over the bath and put his hand in. "No it's not," he said. "It's just right. A bit cool, if anything. Come on. Get your clothes off."

Denzil shrank into a corner, clutched the dressing-gown close, and shook his head. He looked terrified. Sam started to laugh.

"Out you go, young lady," said Travis, pushing her out. "This isn't a public spectacle." He shut the door firmly.

Denzil's bath may not have been a public

spectacle, but the sound effects from it were broadcast throughout the neighbourhood. For twenty minutes Denzil argued, pleaded, made promises, bribed, and begged, but Travis made him undress and get in. Denzil crouched in the bath, clinging to the edge, screaming and swearing that he'd turn himself into a dragon and burn Travis to bits. Travis said he'd dunk the dragon's head underwater and drown the flames. Denzil started shrieking something about scales and great lungs of fire, but Travis knocked his legs out from under him, and Denzil shot underwater. The spell was lost in a fury of bubbles and soap. When Denzil came up again he started howling, begging Travis for mercy, but Travis was far too busy with the soap and face cloth to worry about mercy. Denzil started chanting spells, but Travis poured shampoo over his head, and the soap got in Denzil's eyes, making him forget all about magic.

Sam sat in the lounge, listening, amazed at

how much noise Denzil was making. The television was turned up loud, but she could still hear him. She heard him scream a string of terrible swear words, and Travis yelled something about washing his mouth out with soap. Denzil screamed another wicked word, and then made a few bubbly sounds. It was fairly quiet after that, except for a lot of splashing and spitting.

Then, to her horror, Sam heard the front door bang. She raced into the hallway and almost collided with her mother who was coming out of the kitchen.

"Mum!" she cried loudly. "You're home early!"

"No need to shout, dear," said her mother. "The meeting isn't tonight, after all. I made a mistake. It's on Tuesday. I felt such a fool, arriving there on the wrong night."

There was a slithering, splashing sound from the bathroom, a loud bang, and someone swore. Mrs MacAllister frowned, and leaned her head against the bathroom door.

"Are you having a bath, Travis?" she called through the closed door.

"Yes," mumbled Travis.

"Why? You had a shower just before dinner."

"I got dirty again," called back Travis. "I fell in a hole in the back lawn."

"Do you realize you've flooded the floor?" asked his mother. "There's water coming out from under the door. What *are* you doing in there? Practising butterfly stroke?"

Travis mumbled something else, and then there was an un-Travis-like giggle. Mrs Mac-Allister shrugged, and went into the lounge.

"I really would appreciate a cup of tea," she said to Sam, sinking wearily into a chair. "It's been quite a day, one way and another."

"You watch TV then, and I'll get it," said Sam, racing off to the kitchen. All the time she was making the tea, she listened, but no more suspicious noises came from the bathroom. She guessed they must be finished by now, and wondered whether Travis would poke Denzil out the bathroom window. She hoped Denzil wouldn't turn himself into a rat, not while Travis was looking. Travis didn't like rats.

She finished making the tea, and took it down the passage towards the lounge. As she passed the bathroom she heard some more splashing, and a gurgling noise as the bath started emptying.

"Here's your tea, Mum," she said, setting the cup and saucer down on the small table near her mother's chair.

At that moment there was a bloodcurdling scream from the bathroom.

"The hole! The hole! I'll be sucked down the hole!"

The splashing sounds became frenzied, and the bathroom door flew open. A small, naked body shot out of the bathroom, tore down the passage and out into the kitchen, where it slipped and fell heavily on the linoleum floor.

Sam froze.

Slowly, Mrs MacAllister stood up. She gave

Sam a hard, questioning look, and went down the passage to the kitchen. There was a puddle on the floor, but no one was there. The door was shut, but the kitchen window was wide open. Mrs MacAllister went over to it, and noticed water on the windowsill. There was something else there, too. A feather. A small green feather. She picked it up, frowning, and turned around. Sam was standing behind her, looking worried and afraid.

"Where did this come from?" her mother asked, holding up the feather.

"A budgie," said Sam, smiling suddenly. She gave a huge sigh of relief. "Just as well the window was open," she added. "He could have flown into the glass and been killed."

"Who?" asked Mrs MacAllister, turning pink and white in turns. "That wasn't a budgie I saw running out of the bathroom, with brown legs and black hair and a bare bottom. It was a boy, Samantha. I think you'd better tell me what's going on."

Travis came into the kitchen, looking anxious and very wet. "Sit down, Mum," he said. "There's something you ought to know."

"No!" cried Sam. "She'll take him to the police! You promised!"

"Who?" asked her mother, looking bewildered. "Who's going to the police?"

"No one," said Sam. "There's been no one here. No one in the bath. No one flew out the window. Did they, Travis?"

Travis sighed, and sat heavily in one of the dining chairs. He bent his head in his hands. "I'm sorry, Sam," he said, "but it's time we told the truth. We can't hide him any longer."

"Hide who?" asked Mrs MacAllister.

"You promised!" wailed Sam. She shot Travis a furious, hurt look, and stormed off to her room.

Travis gave his mother a tense smile, and told her all about Denzil.

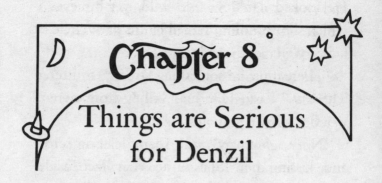

Chapter 8

Things are Serious for Denzil

Theresa's boyfriend parked his car in the drive beside the MacAllisters' house, and turned the motor off. The headlights were still on, and shone straight into the open garage. He saw Mr MacAllister's bike beside the red car, and swore softly.

"Your dad's home early," he said, turning the car lights off. "I'd better not come in."

His black eyebrows came together in a deep frown, and he pushed back his shoulder-length hair and rubbed his beard thoughtfully. His black leather clothes squeaked as he moved, and filled the car with a pleasant, earthy smell. He looked daredevil and wild, yet his eyes – which shone violet, framed by his dark circle of hair – were gentle and warm.

"There must be something wrong," muttered Theresa. "I can hear him yelling from here. I wonder what it's about this time?"

"Not us, anyway," said Adam, leaning across and kissing her. She turned her face aside, frowning, and he kissed her ear instead.

"He probably *is* yelling about us," she said, gloomily. "He doesn't like you, Adam. I don't know what we can do about it, apart from buying you a new wardrobe, taking off your tattoos, shaving your beard, and cutting your hair."

"And throwing out my jewellery," he added, fingering the silver chains about his neck. "He doesn't appreciate my jewellery."

"That reminds me," she said, putting her hand in her skirt pocket and taking something out. "I found this today, in Sam's treehouse.

She's always helping herself to stuff from my room, so I thought I'd get even."

She held up a medallion on a leather thong. The medallion swung and spun slowly in the moonlight, flashing silver on one side and gold on the other. "I thought you might like this," she said, smiling.

"It's beautiful." He was pleased. "Strange, isn't it? Look – there's a little catch on the side, here." He pressed the catch with his fingernail, and the two medallion halves flew open. He took out a lock of hair glimmering silver-blue in the night's light. "Holy Moses!" he breathed, winding the lock of hair around his forefinger, and sniffing it. "It's human hair. An old person's hair."

"It's lovely, isn't it?" said Theresa. "I suppose Sam bought it at a garage sale somewhere. She's always picking up bits of junk. But that's different."

Adam coiled the hair back into the silver half, snapped the medallion shut, and put the leather thong over his mane of dark hair. He tucked the medallion inside his leather vest next to his skin, where it felt smooth and strangely warm and clinked against the silver chains.

"Thanks," he said, kissing her again. "I like it. It's special."

They kissed for a while, until Theresa thought she heard a scratching sound on the car windscreen. She opened her eyes and looked over Adam's shoulder.

"Look – there's a budgie on the car!" she said, laughing. "I wonder where it came from." They watched it for a while, then Theresa grew uneasy. "There's something weird about that bird," she murmured. "It's watching us. It's just perching there, watching. Make it go away, Adam. I don't like it."

The budgie was watching them, its head cocked on one side, its beak pressed against the glass.

"Buzz off!" said Adam, tapping the glass with his finger. The budgie got a bit flustered, but didn't move away. Adam leaned forward and turned on the windscreen wipers. The budgie was knocked aside, and slithered ungracefully off the edge of the bonnet. It was back in a second, looking ruffled and upset.

"What did you do that for?" it squawked. Then it flew off in the direction of the big pine tree at the far end of the garden.

Adam blinked in disbelief. "Did you hear that? The thing talked!"

"It's giving me the creeps," Theresa said, shuddering. "I'm going inside. Do you want to come in for a coffee?"

"Only if I don't have to talk to your old man," said Adam. "If he's rude to me again, I might be tempted to give him a knuckle sandwich."

"No you won't," she said, getting out of the car. "Prove to him that you're a gentleman with class, with an appreciation of fine things and excellent taste."

"I thought I had proved it," grinned Adam, "when I asked his daughter out."

Theresa smiled sweetly, kissed his cheek, and they went inside.

The whole family was in the kitchen, arguing. Sam was in the middle of the uproar, sitting at the table looking sulky and determined.

"You should have known better!" her father shouted. "You've been sheltering a criminal, do you realize that? The little devil could've cleaned out half of the houses in the street. I want to talk to him, right now. Go out to your treehouse and get him."

"He's not here, Dad," said Travis quietly. "That's what I've been trying to tell you. He's gone."

"He's a budgie," said Sam.

"We saw a budgie," said Adam, from the open doorway.

Mr MacAllister glared at him. "What are you doing here?" he growled.

"Reporting on your birdlife," said Adam. "There's a green budgie outside, if you're interested."

"I'm not," said Mr MacAllister. "What I am interested in is a skinny little vandal with black hair and no clothes on."

"There's one of those running across our lawn," said Theresa, looking out behind her.

"Come in and shut the door," said her mother, firmly. "And no more stories, please. We've had enough for one night from Sam, without you starting."

"There is!" cried Theresa.

"That's enough," said her father. "I'd keep pretty quiet if I were you, especially with that great hairy gorilla drooling down your neck. Why isn't it at the zoo?"

"There's no need to be rude," murmured Mrs MacAllister. "How are you, Adam?"

"Fine thanks, Mrs Mac," replied Adam, with a charming smile.

"Would you like a cup of tea?" asked Mrs MacAllister. "I think it's time we all had supper, and calmed down a bit. There's nothing else we can do about that awful Denzil child tonight. With a bit of luck he's gone home and we can forget about him."

At that moment the door from the passage was flung open, and Denzil burst into the kitchen. He was wearing Travis's black silk dressing-gown, with Theresa's pink tights underneath. But he looked so wild-eyed and distraught that no one laughed.

"Someone took it!" he wailed, rushing up to Sam and gripping her arms. "It's gone! Valvasor's going to kill me, if I don't find it! And if I don't find it, I'll never get back!"

He was hurting Sam's arms, and she pulled away from him, alarmed. "What's lost?" she asked. "Your spell?"

"Worse than that!" he cried, anguished. "The magic charm! He'll kill me, I know he will!"

Mr MacAllister went over to Denzil and put his hand on the boy's shoulder, gently. "Nobody's going to kill you, lad," he said, gently. "If your father's cruel to you, no one's going to force you to go back to him. There's special protection for children like you. Now sit down, and tell us about it."

Denzil sat down, shivering with fear. He looked so white and sick that Sam wondered if she should get him a bowl. Her father sat facing Denzil, and asked him questions. His voice was unusually soft and gentle, and for the first time Sam realized just how serious Denzil's situation was.

"What's your name, lad?" asked Mr Mac-Allister.

"Denzil."

"Denzil what? There's no need to be scared. We won't hurt you."

"Denzil. Just Denzil."

Mr MacAllister sighed. "All right. That'll do for the moment. Who's your father?"

"Haven't got one," said Denzil.

"Who's your mother, then?"

"Haven't got one of those, either."

"Who looks after you?"

"Valvasor."

"Where does he live?"

"He's in London Town, buying a new wand."

"Who are you staying with in the meantime?"

"You."

Mr MacAllister was taken aback for a second. Fortunately, his wife put a cup of tea in his hands, and he calmed down a bit while he sipped it. Then he continued: "All right, Denzil, you can stay with us tonight. But I really need to know who you are."

Denzil relaxed slightly. He could see by now that this fierce man with the wild black hair and grim face wasn't really dangerous. And there was something reassuring about having people standing quietly around him, all wanting to help. He was still in deadly trouble over losing the charm with Noah's beard, but he wasn't panicking about it any more. After all, he was a wizard, and a good one. He'd work something out.

"Tell me who you are, lad," the man was saying again.

Denzil stood up, squared his thin shoulders, hitched up his pink ballet tights, and announced grandly: "I'm Denzil, apprentice to Valvasor, the greatest wizard since Merlin."

Mr MacAllister's cup started to rattle in the saucer, and his face went a motley shade of red. Denzil thought he was impressed.

"You've heard of Merlin?" he cried, excited. "He was Valvasor's grandfather! He taught my master everything he knew, and now Valvasor's teaching me! I'm good, too. Really good."

"He is good, Dad," said Sam eagerly. "He's terrific at turning himself into animals. He's not much good at maths, though. Or tidying up."

"Or telling the truth," said her father heavily, his fierce eyes still on Denzil's face. "Sit down, Denzil, and start again. And this time, tell the truth."

Denzil perched on the edge of his chair, and swallowed nervously. "I'm Denzil," he said solemnly, "apprentice to the mighty Valvasor. Merlin wasn't really his grandfather. I just said that to make it sound good. Actually, Valvasor's grandfather was a falcon called Zathar. That's why we're such good flyers. We were taught by the best."

Mr MacAllister choked on his tea. He spluttered for a while, then said hoarsely: "My patience is running out, Denzil."

Denzil gulped. "I'm being as true as I know how, my lord," he said, earnestly. "I live in Northwood Village, second cottage on the right. At least, it's on the right if you come from the windmill, and on the left if you come from the duckpond. It's called Northwood because it's north of the Great Wood where Sir Godric goes fox hunting. And he hunts deer too, of course, because every Michaelmas he holds these big feasts, and it's like a surprise because—"

"You'll get a surprise in a minute," hissed Mr MacAllister, "right across your backside. Now start telling the truth!"

Denzil's eyes filled with tears, and he clasped his hands pleadingly. "Please, my lord. I'm telling the truth. Honest. And you can't make me go home, not until I've finished my sums and worked out all the calculations, and figured out when Spy Wednesday is, and found the magic charm. I can't go till then."

He choked, and tears poured down his cheeks. "I'm doing my best, but I'm not that good at sums. That's how I ended up here. And Valvasor's going to get murdered by a dragon." He started to howl loudly, writhing on the chair, and wringing his hands in desperation. "Oh, sweet Jesus have mercy! Saint Christopher preserve me! I'm doomed! I'm doomed!"

"Good Lord – he's a better actor than I am!" murmured Mr MacAllister, impressed.

"He's not acting," said Sam. "He really is a wizard! Ask him to do a spell! Go on!"

"Don't be silly, Samantha," said Mrs Mac-Allister. She went over to Denzil and put her arms around his trembling shoulders. "It's all right, my darling," she crooned, lovingly. "No one's going to hurt you. We'll help you get home, I promise. Hush, now. Don't cry any more, your nose is dripping all over Theresa's tights."

"I *thought* those were mine!" cried Theresa angrily, going over and frowning down at Denzil. "It was you in my room today, not Sam! You little thief!"

Her words had an amazing effect on Denzil. He shot up out of Mrs MacAllister's arms, his face transformed by fury. "I'm not a thief!" he screamed. "I'm not!"

"What are you then?" asked Theresa.

Denzil puffed out his chest, looked as important as he could, and said proudly, "I'm a burglar."

"Same thing," said Theresa.

"It's not!" shouted Denzil, his face purple

with rage. "Thieves are sneaky and low. They're villains. But burglars are different. Burglars are brave and bold. They have – have . . ." He groped for the right word.

"Class," said Adam, helpfully. "Excellent taste, and an appreciation of fine things. Like me."

Denzil nodded.

"Whether you're a thief or a burglar isn't important," said Mr MacAllister, sternly. "You're still in the wrong. You can't just go into people's houses and take their property. You can't run away from home, either."

"Not until you're my age," said Theresa pointedly.

Mr MacAllister ignored her. "I'm afraid I'm going to have to call the police, Denzil," he went on, quietly. "Your parents must have reported you missing hours ago. They'll have your name on the police computer."

He got up and went over to the phone.

Denzil, having no idea who the police were

or what the phone was, wasn't worried at all. But Sam went berserk.

"You can't call the police!" she howled, dragging on her father's arm. "Don't, Dad! They'll put him in prison! He'll never be able to finish his sums! He'll be stuck here forever!"

Denzil understood the bit about forever. He screamed and made a dash for the window, but Travis grabbed him. "No, you don't!" Travis said, pinning Denzil's arms behind him. "You're not getting away again!"

"Wings of bats and acrobats, bring me fledgling—" began Denzil, but Travis clapped his hand over Denzil's mouth.

"You're talking nonsense, Denzil," he said calmly. "Acrobats don't have wings. Now keep still and behave yourself while we sort this out."

Denzil fought and kicked and tried to bite Travis's hand. He accidentally kicked Mrs Mac-Allister in the stomach, and she cried out and bent over, moaning. Adam rushed to her side, and supported her with his arm.

"Get your hands off my wife!" roared Mr MacAllister, taking a swing at Adam's jaw. He missed, and his fist went smashing into a cupboard door. He gave a howl of rage and pain.

There was a knock on the back door, and Sam answered it. It was Mrs Utherwise, smiling sweetly, and pretending this kind of bedlam went on all the time in every family. "May I have a cup of milk, dearie?" she asked. "I'm making some custard tarts, and I've run out of milk."

"Sure," said Sam, going to the fridge and taking out a carton only half full. She walked back through her howling family, past Denzil, still fighting like a wild thing with his head clamped under Travis's elbow, and gave Mrs Utherwise the milk. She apologized for all the noise. "It's because of Denzil," Sam explained. "Dad's going to call the police, and they'll take him away."

"Oh dear," clucked Mrs Utherwise, shaking her head like a concerned hen. "I suppose Weasel doesn't want to go?"

"Not to prison," said Sam. "He wants to go to Spy Wednesday, and warn Valvasor about a dragon." She sighed. "I wish Dad wouldn't phone the police," she added. "I wish our phone wouldn't work."

"I suppose that would be a help," murmured Mrs Utherwise, thoughtfully. Then she smiled cheerfully and left.

"Who was that?" asked Theresa, helping Adam get Mrs MacAllister onto a chair, where she sat, moaning and gasping.

"It was Mrs Utherwise, from the house across the road," said Sam, watching her father pick up the phone book and look up the number. He was sucking his knuckles, which were bleeding.

"There's no one there," said Theresa, irritably. "The house is still for sale. I wish you wouldn't make things up all the time, Samantha."

Mr MacAllister dialled the number and waited, frowning. Then he shook his head, puzzled, and dialled again. "That's funny," he said. "The phone's suddenly gone dead." He dialled again, carefully, then hung up. He looked at Denzil. "You'll have to stay here for the night, after all," he said, "if you can stop kicking long enough to get into a bed."

"Westward wind and buzzards skinned, speed me on to where I'm destined," chanted Denzil, then stopped. "What? Can I stay and finish my sums?"

"Yes," said Mr MacAllister. "Let him go, Travis."

Denzil ducked out from under Travis's arm, hitched up his tights again, and straightened his dressing-gown. "I'll retire to the tree house, then," he said, with a dignified air. "I'll sleep with Murgatroyd. But I'd be obliged if you'd give me supper first."

"Oh, you poor little thing," Mrs MacAllister murmured. "Haven't they fed you yet?"

"I'll heat him up some baked beans," said Travis. "You sit there and rest, Mum. That was a nasty kick you got. You're lucky he didn't rupture something. And it's time you went to bed, Sam. It's ten o'clock. I saw you yawning before."

"I'm not tired," said Sam, covering another yawn with her hand. "I want to help Denzil do his sums."

"I'll help him tomorrow," said Travis, putting a saucepan on the stove. "I wasn't too bad at maths when I was at school."

Denzil sat at the table and folded his arms. "Go and get my sums, Samantha," he commanded.

"Get them yourself," said Sam, and Denzil looked shocked.

"You get to bed, Sam," said her mother. "You've got school in the morning. You'll never wake up in time."

"I'll get the sums first," said Sam, and raced out before they could stop her. She was back a few minutes later, with piles of pages that looked as if they'd been torn out of books. She dumped them all on the table in front of Denzil, and gave him a ballpoint pen.

He looked at the pen mystified, and made a mark on the paper with it. "Nice," he said. "Better than a quill." He tipped it upside-down and waited for all the ink to run out.

Everyone leaned over the papers on the table, and Theresa picked up a long poem. "Time of tomorrow," she read aloud. "Hours of today, Trackless and—"

"Gawd, you can't read that!" yelled Denzil, snatching the spell away. "You'll disappear!"

"Let her read it, then," said Sam, with an impish smile.

Denzil put the spell in his dressing-gown pocket, and looked through the pages of sums.

"I've got to figure out how many days there are back to Spy Wednesday in the year 1291," he said. "And then I've got to divide that by the number of miles a crow flies in an hour, and multiply it by the exact time the sun's in its zenith. I've also got to calculate the number of miles to London Town."

"You're having us on, aren't you?" said Mr MacAllister. "This sounds like a mathematician's nightmare. Why don't you take up something easy, like brain surgery?"

Adam was leaning over Denzil's papers, arranging them in order. Mr MacAllister made a scornful sound. "It'll be more than your brain cell can cope with," he said. "Why don't you just go home and peel yourself a banana?"

Adam pointed at some of Denzil's figures, his face frowning and intent. Then he rubbed his beard thoughtfully. "You need to apply Einstein's theory of relativity here," he said to Denzil. "You haven't taken into account the fact that energy put out by time is oscillating. Time alters between cause and effect. Therefore the calculations at the beginning of your journey are different from the calculations at the end.

"And you're into subatomic mathematics, when you go back. Don't forget that. And the crow's out of date, now. You'll need to divide this time by the speed of light. You used a medieval quadrant for working this bit out, didn't you? It's not accurate enough, Denzil, not for the distances you're working with. I've got a computer at home. I'll bring it round tomorrow when I've finished work."

Denzil looked slightly confused, but he nodded.

Mr MacAllister blinked. "You know a bit about maths, Adam?" he asked.

Adam grinned. "I've got a degree in maths and physics," he said.

Mr MacAllister went red in the face but he said nothing.

Denzil smiled up at Adam. He liked this clever, wild-looking man. He wondered if he was a rogue or a highwayman, and that was why Mr Mac didn't like him. "Reckon we'll work it all out, then, Adam?" Denzil asked.

"No trouble at all," said Adam. "By this time tomorrow, you'll be all set to take off."

Chapter 9

Seeing Stars

The next day, Friday, Mr MacAllister stayed home and kept a wary eye on Denzil. He still suspected that Denzil had told a string of lies and was quietly plotting a burglary campaign across the whole neighbourhood. He intended to watch Denzil closely, every moment.

He didn't need to worry. Denzil had discovered the television, and sat open-mouthed and enthralled in front of it – burglary, his sums, Valvasor, Spy Wednesday and the dragon all forgotten. All morning he watched the astounding world inside the shining box. He shrieked with laughter at the news and the scientific documentaries, cheered and screamed at the sports programmes, and sobbed over the cartoons. In the afternoon Mr MacAllister decided to give him a treat, and hired the video of *Star Wars*.

Denzil watched the first ten minutes without a sound, without moving, almost without breathing. Mr MacAllister sat and watched Denzil. Denzil was rapt, his eyes out on stalks. Suddenly he fled, screaming, into Mr Mac-Allister's arms and watched the rest of the movie from there, trembling with terror and amazement and adoration. By the end of it, Mr MacAllister was convinced Denzil had never seen a television before, let alone a robot or a spaceship.

"You're a strange one, aren't you?" he said gently, when the movie was over. "It's not true, you know, Denzil. None of that really happened. You do realize that? It was all acting, make-up, costumes and trick photography."

Denzil sighed dreamily. He couldn't speak, not even to ask what photography was. He had just seen a whole new world, and the hugeness and wonder of it had blown his old world to smithereens. He felt as if his brain had been taken out, stretched across the universe, then screwed up and poked back into his skull again.

Sam arrived home from school and couldn't get any sense out of Denzil at all. He kept staring into space and muttering things about stars, great chariots that flew, and knights who fought with swords of light. After a while Sam gave up talking to him and went to a friend's house.

Adam arrived with the computer, and Mr MacAllister helped him set it up on the kitchen table. Denzil watched, silent, still in a daze. When it was all ready, Adam shot Denzil a wide grin. "Where are your sums, Denzil?" he asked. "We'll get these calculations sorted out, and then you can go home."

"Don't want to," said Denzil in a dreamy voice. "I want to go to the galaxy."

Adam stared at him, surprised. "What? You don't want to go home? What about Valvasor, and that animal that's after him? What about all your friends?"

Denzil shook his head and smiled. His face was flushed, and his eyes had stars in them. "The galaxy," he repeated.

Adam stared helplessly at Mr MacAllister. "What's he on about?" he asked. "I didn't think they even knew about the galaxy, where he comes from."

"*Star Wars*," said Mr MacAllister with a grin. "I showed him the video of *Star Wars*."

"What a stupid thing to do!" burst out Adam. "He's from the Middle Ages! He's never seen anything more exciting than a parade or a performing bear! What are you trying to do – knock him out in one afternoon with seven hundred years of science and technology? You'll blow his brain apart!"

"It was only a film!" yelled Mr MacAllister. "He was only sitting on a chair watching a film! I didn't let him go flying an airliner!"

Adam sighed, and glanced down at Denzil. Denzil was staring at the computer screen, fascinated. "Will I see the galaxy again?" he asked, hopefully.

"You'll see everything you're supposed to see," said Adam firmly. "Just go and get your sums, and I'll show you magic like you've never seen before."

Denzil did as he was told, and for a while he and Adam worked together at the computer. But every five minutes Denzil asked where the stars and spaceships were. Adam made excuses and vague promises, and glared sideways at Mr MacAllister.

Mr MacAllister reddened, looking sheepish and guilty. He soon stopped watching, and began to prepare dinner.

Because the computer was on the dining table,

and there were piles of printouts, sums and spells on the kitchen floor, the family had dinner in the lounge, sitting with their plates on their knees. Adam had been invited to stay for the meal. He sat beside Theresa on the sofa and they held hands while they ate, which was difficult because they had to cut their steaks with their forks.

Denzil sat beside Travis, picking the beans out of his salad and dropping them on the floor. Joplin crouched at his feet, gobbling up the beans as fast as Denzil dropped them.

"Don't do that, please, Denzil," said Mrs MacAllister, softly. "If you don't like the salad, leave it on the side of your plate. And please use your knife and fork."

"I like the salad," said Denzil. "I like onion. It's the beans I don't like. And forks are silly. They're not natural." His eyes stole across the room to the television. "Can we make it come alive again?" he asked. "Please?"

"All right," said Mr MacAllister, getting up. "It's time for the news, anyway."

"Leave it off," said Adam.

Mr MacAllister stopped halfway across the room, and stared back at Adam with narrowed eyes. "Are you ordering me around in my own home?" he asked.

Adam nodded, and his earrings swung, glinting, above his silver chains. He jerked his fork in Denzil's direction. "You've done enough damage to him already," he said. "Show him any more modern stuff, and you'll have the knights driving to the crusades in cars before they've even discovered petrol."

"What do you mean?" asked Mr MacAllister.

"Who's got a pet troll?" asked Denzil, amazed.

"See what I mean?" grinned Adam. "Leave him in the Middle Ages, Mr Mac. You could mess up history. It's bad enough that the kid's using a knife and fork, let alone seeing things that in his world haven't even been invented. Let's keep his life simple."

Mr MacAllister nodded and sat down again,

and Denzil howled to have the television on.

"Any more of that, Denzil, and you won't get any ice-cream," warned Mrs MacAllister.

Denzil howled louder.

"Shut up. You sound like a girl," said Travis. Denzil was instantly quiet. Sam gave Travis a furious look and he grinned at her and winked.

"It's a pity not to entertain Denzil some-how," murmured Mr MacAllister. "I mean, he's like a visitor from overseas, isn't he? We should show him around a bit, while he's here."

"Just be careful what you do show him," warned Adam. "He's seven hundred years behind us, don't forget."

"I'm not a fool," said Denzil, haughtily. "Bet I can do spells better than you, even with your fancy computer."

"What sort of things do you like, Denzil?" asked Mr MacAllister. "Puppet shows, play things, things like that?"

"Oh, they're nothing, now," said Denzil, his eyes on the television. Then his face lit up. "I like battles," he said. "I saw an army once. All King Edward's men, marching off to stop a Welsh revolt. Grand they were, with their bows and swords flashing in the sun."

"Bloodthirsty little blighter," murmured Travis, with a smile. "Maybe we should let you watch the TV news, after all. Modern war would blow you away."

Denzil's fork skidded across his plate, showering beans all over Joplin. He threw the fork on the floor and picked up his steak in his fingers. "I like travelling players," he said, tearing the steak in half. "I like acrobats and minstrels and actors."

"Do you now?" asked Mr MacAllister, leaning forward, interested. "I'm an actor. Or I was. There's no work for me any more."

"Why? Did they throw rotten eggs at you?" grinned Denzil.

Mr MacAllister smiled. "No. I wish that's all it was. We didn't make enough money. It costs a lot to keep a theatre going. And the government doesn't help."

"They've got theatres in London Town," Denzil informed them with his mouth full. "Valvasor told me."

"Shakespeare's theatre?" cried Mr Mac-Allister, excited, forgetting that he didn't believe anything Denzil said. "Valvasor's seen Shakespeare?"

Denzil shrugged, and wiped his chin on his sleeve. "Never heard of Shakespeare," he said. "Is he a soldier, good at shaking a spear?"

Mr MacAllister groaned.

"Denzil's from 1291," explained Adam. "Shakespeare's later."

"I know when Shakespeare was born," growled Mr MacAllister. "But I'm still not sure about Denzil. I reckon he's having us on. Laughing at us up his black silk sleeves, I bet. Aren't you, Denzil?"

Denzil shook his head. "No. But I'd laugh if you did some acting," he said. "Be a jester for me?"

"Go on, darling," urged Mrs MacAllister. "You were marvellous at comedy. You used to have the audience in fits."

Mr MacAllister smiled. "Well . . . I could put on a one-man show, I suppose. I could do that play about the king's court jester."

"Perfect!" said Adam.

"That was fantastic!" cried Sam, excited. "I loved that play! Will you do it for us, Dad? Please?"

Mr MacAllister's face lit up. "Actually, I'd love to," he said. "It'd be great to perform again."

"We could have it at the weekend," said Mrs MacAllister, eagerly. "On Sunday. Sam could invite her friends, and make a special morning of it."

"I'll make some popcorn," said Sam.

"I'll paint the scenery," said Travis.

"I'll make the jester's performing bear," said Denzil.

"He doesn't have a bear," said Sam. Denzil's face fell.

Mr MacAllister looked at his watch. "I've got to go to work," he said, jumping up. He kissed Mrs MacAllister and rushed out.

"He hasn't looked this happy for ages," Mrs MacAllister said, smiling to herself. "It's a marvellous idea to put on a play. He could be acting every weekend, doing what he loves. Why didn't we think of this before?" She glanced across the room at Denzil and her smile widened. "You're good for this family, Denzil," she added. "You've made Mr Mac appreciate Adam's good points, and you've shown him a way to do his acting again. You've made us all pull together. I wish we could keep you."

Denzil gave her an angelic smile, and wondered why everyone else groaned.

Chapter 10

Problems and Surprises

Adam was at the MacAllisters' house by nine o'clock on Saturday morning, to continue working on the computer. He was having problems with Denzil's calculations. He knew he had to send Denzil back seven hundred years, to Spy Wednesday in the year 1291. But Denzil didn't know the date for Spy Wednesday. He didn't even know which month it was in.

To Denzil, the time of year was just summer or winter, autumn or spring. To him special times were called Harvest-tide, Twelfth Night,

Candlemas, Valentine's Day, or Christmas. He didn't know that Christmas was on the twenty-fifth day of December, or that New Year's Day was the first day of January. He knew only that they were special days, when everyone feasted and got drunk. He didn't count the days or the weeks, or know the names of the months. So he couldn't tell Adam anything except that he had to go back to the year 1291, and to the day called Spy Wednesday.

To finish the calculations and write the correct answers into Denzil's spell, Adam needed an exact date. So he went to the library and looked through books on medieval history. He read about Plough Monday, Shrove Tuesday and Ash Wednesday – but he found nothing about Spy Wednesday. He came home again and asked Denzil questions, trying to find clues.

"Is Spy Wednesday in the winter?" he asked.

Denzil screwed up his face and thought hard. "Well, it's cold," he said, "but it's getting warm. It could be a cold day in summer, or a warm day in winter. I'm not sure, really."

"That's a lot of help," said Adam. "Is Spy Wednesday after Christmas?"

"Everything's after Christmas," said Denzil, "until it's nearly the next Christmas, and then it's before."

"Is it soon after Christmas?" asked Adam.

Denzil shook his head.

"Is it before May Day?"

Denzil nodded.

"How many days before May Day?" asked Adam.

"Lots," said Denzil.

"Is it before Valentine's Day?"

Denzil looked blank. Then his face lit up and he cried helpfully, "It's just before church! We all go to church and the bells ring like mad, and we wear clean clothes, and the sun dances in the sky, and the king washes everyone's dirty feet!"

"Well, that's a help," muttered Adam, doubtfully. "We're obviously into some very obscure medieval custom – one that involves getting clean. No wonder you call it a special day. But why call it Spy Wednesday?"

"Judas," said Denzil gravely. "We remember Judas, the spy."

"Judas wasn't a spy, Denzil. He was a disciple."

"He was a spy!" shouted Denzil, starting to go red in the face. "Lord, you're dumb! Don't they tell you anything in church?"

"I don't go that often," admitted Adam. "But I do know that Judas wasn't a spy."

"He was! He was! He spied on Wednesday, and—"

"All right, don't get excited. Yelling and screaming won't help. Obviously you've got your wires crossed, or you're talking about a different Judas. A long-forgotten saint, probably, with a talent for spying on people on their annual bath day."

Denzil looked sulky and hurt, and Adam slipped an arm around the boy's shoulders.

"I'm sorry. But remembering vague customs isn't good enough. We have to know the exact date of Spy Wednesday in the year 1291, and then I can work out exactly how far back to send you. I need a date, Denzil. Any old day in 1291 won't do. You have to go back to Spy Wednesday and warn that Valvasor guy about whatever it is that's going to kill him."

"A dragon," said Denzil, gravely. "That's what's going to get him."

"Yes. Well, it's probably some kind of poisonous snake," said Adam.

"It's a dragon," said Denzil. "A one-eyed dragon with huge long claws. It's long and black, and goes roaring through the night."

"Sounds terrible," said Adam, leaning over the computer again.

"Mother Wyse warned me about it," said Denzil, peering over Adam's shoulder, and watching him tap in some more information. "She's a witch."

"Has she got a black cat?" asked Adam,

frowning at the screen.

"Yes. And a black bird."

"And she flies on a broomstick, I suppose?"

"They say she does, but I haven't seen her. You know a bit about witches, do you?"

Adam smiled. "I was taught by one, at school," he said. "Are you sure you can't remember how many days there are between Spy Wednesday and Christmas? That really would be a huge help."

Denzil shook his head. His eyes took on a strange gleam, and he said, eagerly: "Adam, since I can't go straight home, I've got some time to spare, haven't I? I could go to the galaxy. Please, Adam. Let me go to the galaxy!"

"You can't," said Adam. "It's not real, Denzil. Not the galaxy you saw, anyway. It was a film. A fantasy. A pretend place. Forget it. You've got more important things to do."

"It *was* real!" cried Denzil, pulling on Adam's arm. "It was in that box when Mr Mac made it come alive! It's in there!" He dragged

Adam into the lounge. Mr MacAllister was watching a game of cricket on television. Denzil rushed over and threw himself at Mr Mac-Allister's feet. "Please," Denzil begged, wringing his hands. "Please, please make the galaxy again."

"I can't," said Mr MacAllister, making Denzil stand up. "I've taken the video back. It's not here, Denzil."

"Yes it is!" howled Denzil, rushing over to the television, and frantically pushing buttons. "It's inside here!"

"Hey – where's my cricket?" yelled Mr Mac-Allister. "Leave it alone, Denzil! You've mucked up the colour!"

"I want the galaxy!" cried Denzil, desperate, clawing at the television screen. Adam hauled him away. Denzil fought and kicked, and Adam gave him a slap on the backside. Denzil looked at him, shocked. Then he sniffed, rearranged his black dressing-gown, and flounced off into Sam's room.

Mr MacAllister gave up, turned off the television, and sat down again. He chewed on his lower lip, and glowered at Adam.

Adam sat down and glowered back. "I wish you hadn't shown him *Star Wars*," said Adam angrily. "Why didn't you show him something he could cope with, like *Snow White* or *Robin Hood*? Something nearer his own time?"

"He's not medieval!" shouted Mr MacAllister, standing up and starting to pace the room. "Do you think I'm crazy, Adam? That kid's a runaway, out of an orphanage somewhere, or a welfare home. He could even be from a special hospital. He's probably not quite all there. There's something funny about him. He's not normal."

"He's very intelligent, actually," said Adam, quietly. "He's excellent at maths, and he's pretty quick at catching on to physics, and the properties and changes of matter and energy. He's got an amazing understanding of the quantum theory."

"He must be brainier than I am then," muttered Mr MacAllister.

"Probably," said Adam.

Mr MacAllister glared at him, and left the room. Adam laughed quietly to himself. He was about to go too, when he heard a scrabbling noise inside the television set. He stopped and listened. The scrabbling and scratching went on, quietly but persistently. "There's a mouse in there!" said Adam to himself. "Poor little thing." He turned the set off at the wall, and called out to Mr MacAllister.

"Hey – Mr Mac! Got a screwdriver? We'll have to take the back off your TV. There's a mouse in there."

Sam came into the lounge, blowing huge bubbles of blue bubblegum. "It's not a mouse," she said. "It's Denzil. He said he was going in there. He's looking for the galaxy."

Adam gave her a pale smile. "You're joking, aren't you, Sam?" he said.

"No," said Sam. She blew an extra large

bubble, which popped all over her face. "He's a wizard. He can turn himself into an animal. I've seen him."

"I can accept that he's travelled through time," said Adam slowly, "but I can't swallow that wizard stuff. That's a bit far-fetched."

Travis came down the passage towards them, a collection of tools in his hands. "Who wanted a screwdriver?" he asked. He'd been working on his motorbike and was wearing overalls covered with oil and grease.

"There's a mouse inside the TV," said Adam. "Sam reckons it's Denzil."

Travis grinned. "Sam's got a terrific imagination," he said, going past them into the lounge. He knelt in front of the television and listened. "I don't hear anything," he said.

Mrs MacAllister came in through the patio door from the garden, her hands full of flowers. "Travis, what are you doing in here in those filthy clothes?" she asked. "Look at your boots. You'll get grease all over the carpet. Get up."

"There's a mouse in here somewhere," said Travis. "It was in the TV."

Mrs MacAllister looked around quickly. "Well, don't let Theresa see it," she warned. "You know she's terrified of mice. We'd better find it." She put the flowers down on the coffee table, and bent to look under the sofa.

"There it is – under that window!" cried Travis, and made a dive for it. He missed the mouse, but got grease all over the cream curtains.

"Oh, Travis!" groaned Mrs MacAllister.

Sam crawled behind the sofa. "He might be behind here," she said.

Theresa came in. She saw Sam and her mother crawling on the floor, and Adam with his head in the fireplace. "What are you looking for?" she asked.

"A needle," said Mrs MacAllister.

"A screw," said Travis.

"A big fat mouse," said Sam.

Theresa screamed and jumped onto the coffee

table, crushing the flowers. "Find it!" she wailed. "I can't live here if there's a mouse!"

"Leave then," said Sam, from under the sofa. "You're always saying you will. There it is, Travis! Quick! Running across the carpet! Oh, you've missed him!"

Theresa screamed again.

"It'll probably go into the pantry," said Adam, "where the food is."

"He won't go anywhere near Joplin," said Sam, crawling out. "He'll probably hide for a while."

"Who'll hide?" asked Denzil, and they all spun around. He was sitting on top of the television. His face looked strange – altered somehow. Strange, long whiskers quivered on his cheeks. Slowly, like a picture coming gradually into focus, he was himself again.

Theresa started screaming, louder than ever. Mrs MacAllister gave a little moan and fainted. Luckily she fell across the sofa and wasn't hurt. Travis went white and abruptly sat down on a chair. Adam went white too, and sat on Mrs MacAllister. Sam went over to Denzil and helped him off the television.

"You shouldn't have done that!"

"I had to," said Denzil, angrily. "And it's all a lie, a trick! There's nothing in there, except junk. There's no spaceship. No stars. No robot. Nothing." He was almost in tears.

Mr MacAllister came in. "What's going on?" he asked, seeing their white faces. "Do stop screaming, Theresa, and get down off that table. Why are you sitting on my wife, Adam? Get off!"

Adam stood up, and Mrs MacAllister moaned. "She fainted," explained Sam. "Denzil turned himself into a mouse."

Mr MacAllister sat on the sofa by his wife, and propped her up with cushions. He held her hands and kissed her cheek. She opened her eyes and groaned again. When he was sure she was all right, Mr MacAllister stood up and went over to Denzil. "I've had enough of you, young man," he said. "You've caused nothing but trouble in this house."

"I didn't mean to," said Denzil. "I wanted to see the galaxy again, so I turned myself into a mouse and looked inside the magic box. It's not there."

"Stop telling lies!" cried Mr MacAllister.

"I'm not lying! It's gone – the galaxy, the spaceship, everything!"

"I meant about you being a mouse!" shouted Mr MacAllister. "This Middle Ages stuff, and you being a wizard, and having no parents – I'm sick of it! I'm warning you, Denzil. One more lie, and I'm calling the police to come and take you away."

"He's not lying, Dad," said Travis in a low voice. "He was still changing back when we saw him. His eyes were weird, and he had little grey hairs all over his face. It was only for a second. Then he was Denzil again. But we saw."

"I'm not stupid!" snarled his father. "If

there's any more of this nonsense, I'm not doing that play. We'll all clean up the garage, instead."

"That's not fair!" wailed Sam. "It's all organized! I've asked all my friends to come. I'm not letting Denzil spoil it."

"I'm not spoiling anything!" cried Denzil.

"Yes you are," said Theresa. "You're spoiling my pink tights, for a start. You've got holes in them. And the other day you tried on my clothes, you drew on my mirror with my lipstick, you poured my perfume all over my potplants, and you *licked* my eyeshadows! You've wasted all this Saturday with my boyfriend, doing your silly sums, and now you're spoiling the play. I hope the police do come and lock you up."

"I'm trying to be good," Denzil whined. "I didn't know all that paint and stuff was for your stupid face!"

"That's enough," said Mrs MacAllister, standing up and leaning shakily on Travis. She didn't seem to notice that she was getting grease all over her dress. "We're all going to have a nice quiet afternoon getting ready for the play, and tomorrow morning we'll have a wonderful time. There won't be any more shouting, strange happenings or surprises. Will there, Denzil?"

Denzil smiled sweetly. "No, Mrs Mac-Allister," he lied.

Chapter 11

A Brilliant Performance

The play was a great success. There were thirty children in the audience, because all Sam's friends had brought their friends as well. Instead of being in the lounge, the play was performed outside on the lawn under Sam's treehouse. As it turned out, it was just as well.

Travis had built and painted the scenery, which was a king's hall in a castle. Denzil, who had never seen a castle but had heard about them, was most impressed. Mr MacAllister had borrowed a court jester's costume. He had painted his face, too, and looked stunning. And his act was amazing.

He did things he didn't know he could do. He sang songs he'd never learned, told jokes he'd never heard before, and performed gymnastic feats that should have crippled him but made him feel great. His audience clapped, cheered, and roared with laughter. But it was his magic that made the day.

He pulled rainbow-coloured ribbons out of the end of a wand, live birds out of his pockets, and silk scarves out of Mrs MacAllister's ears. He took golden rings, connected them all together in a long, unbreakable chain, and then made them separate again. He juggled coloured balls, which fell apart and showered him with glittering silver stars. He covered stones with magic scarves, and when he pulled the scarves away the stones burst into fantastic flowers. He pulled ducklings out of coloured boxes, green flames out of bottles, and a fierce-looking falcon out of a black top hat. He spun plates on sticks, and the plates turned into silver starships with winking lights, and flew up into the blue.

Mr MacAllister nearly died of shock, but his audience cheered with delight.

Sam glanced at Denzil, sitting quietly beside her. "He's never done anything that good before," she said. But Denzil didn't hear. He was watching her father closely, frowning, his unusual green eyes burning with strange lights. "Denzil?" said Sam, suspiciously. "Denzil? What are you doing?"

Suddenly the audience around her gasped with amazement, and Sam looked back at her father. He was wearing a long black robe with a dark hood, and seemed to be having trouble walking. Suddenly he flung off the black robe, and they saw that he had turned into a shining golden robot, jerky and surprised, and making startled bleeping noises. The children squealed with joy.

Sam looked at Denzil again. He looked back and grinned. "Beautiful, isn't he?" he said.

"Don't get too clever," Sam whispered. "You'll have every kid in the school over here tomorrow, wanting to see this. Mum'll have a fit."

Denzil nodded gravely, and when Sam looked back at her father, he was himself again.

The performance finished soon after that. Everyone went home shouting words like "Choice!", "Fantastic!", and "Terrific!"

Mr MacAllister was flushed with pleasure and satisfaction. "That was the best time I've had in my whole life," he said later, when they were having lunch. "I don't know how I did it."

"Brilliantly," said Mrs MacAllister, leaning over and kissing him. "You did it brilliantly. I didn't know you could do all those tricks."

"Neither did I," he grinned, helping himself to a big piece of cake. "Reckon I've got some talents I didn't know I had." He looked at Denzil, and his grin widened. "I bet I gave you a few surprises, young lad. You look worn out. Overwhelmed by it all, are you?"

Denzil smiled. He did look tired, and Sam

suddenly realized that doing magic was hard work. He was only a young wizard, after all.

"I think Denzil was terrific," she said.

"What did Denzil have to do with it?" asked her father. "Helped paint the scenery, did he?"

"I expect he had more to do with it than you think," murmured Mrs MacAllister, smiling to herself.

"Well, I hope you've got some energy left, Denzil," said Adam, pushing back his chair. "Because we've got to work on those sums again this afternoon."

Denzil groaned. "I want to go to some other places first," he said.

"What places, Denzil?" asked Theresa. "To the shops maybe, to buy me some new make-up? And tights, to replace the ones you stole?"

"To the galaxy," said Denzil.

Mr MacAllister rubbed his chin, thoughtfully. "Isn't it funny," he said, wonderingly, "how we just saw that film, then I accidentally got mixed up with that robot costume? And those plates, flying off into space like that. I didn't know I could do that. I must be cleverer than I thought."

"I'm sure you're a genius," grinned Adam. "Maybe you could do Denzil's sums for him. What do you know about quantum energy and subatomic mathematics?"

"Everything," said Mr MacAllister, getting up and starting to clear the table. "But I'd hate to deprive your brain of a bit of exercise. We'll do the dishes, and you and Denzil can get back to the computer. Maybe you'll have it all worked out by tonight, and Denzil can go home. There's a slim chance his parents are missing him."

But they didn't have it worked out by that night. Or the next night. And Adam was getting worried.

When Sam came home from school on Tuesday, her father was weeding the vegetable garden. She went over to him, swinging her schoolbag, and he stood up. "Hi, Sam," he said. "How was school today?"

"All right," she replied. "But I wish I could have stayed at home with Denzil. Has he finished his sums yet?"

"No." Her father frowned and bent to pull up a dandelion he'd missed. "There's something funny about that kid," he said. "Adam took the whole day off work to carry on with those calculations, and all Denzil can do is sit in front of the TV and eat crisps. The way he scoffs them, you'd think he'd never had them before."

"He hasn't," said Sam.

"He says now he doesn't want to go home," said her father. "He wants to live with us."

"He could live in my treehouse," said Sam eagerly. "It's a bit of a mess since Theresa drew on the walls and tore down the curtains, but Denzil won't mind. He likes a mess."

"So I've noticed," grinned her father, kneeling down again and continuing his weeding. "He's a strange kid, all right. I phoned the police this morning to see if anyone had reported a missing boy. No one had. It's really strange. Maybe his parents are glad to be rid of him. It's sad, really. He's a nice kid. I wouldn't mind adopting him if he didn't make so much fuss over having a bath."

Sam smiled, hugged him about the neck, and went into the house. Adam was sitting at the dining table, staring at the computer screen. He looked tired and fed up. "Hello, Sam," he said. "How's it going?"

"All right," she replied, going into the pantry. "Where are all the gingernuts?"

"Denzil ate them," said Adam. "I've never seen a kid eat the way he does. I reckon he was starved before he came here. Maybe there was a famine in 1291."

Sam picked up an apple instead, and went into her room. She dropped her schoolbag onto the floor, then joined Denzil in the lounge. He was crouched in front of the television, sniffing it. There was a programme on about farming pigs.

"It's not true," said Denzil, sniffing hard. "There's no smell. All pigs smell. I know. We've got pigs at home. We cut their heads off, slit them open, take out all their bones, and boil them."

Sam collapsed into a chair and munched on her apple. "You're not allowed to watch TV that close," she said. "It's bad for your eyes."

Denzil ignored her. There were pieces of potato crisps all over the carpet, and Joplin had his head in the empty bag, licking up the salty remains.

"Do you want to come and play in the tree-house?" asked Sam.

Denzil shook his head, and went on sniffing.

"Do you want to come and play at Janey's?"

"No."

"What do you want to do then?"

"Go to the galaxy."

Sam sighed. She stood up and went outside. Mrs Utherwise was on her front veranda, feeding her bird. She saw Sam and waved, and Sam went over to talk to her. Joplin went too, looking for trouble.

In the kitchen, Adam turned the computer off and put the kettle on for a cup of coffee. He opened the pantry door and took out some food to make himself a sandwich. Denzil heard the sound of food being prepared, and came out.

"Have you finished my sums yet?" he asked, poking his fingers into the butter, then licking them.

"No, I haven't," said Adam, testily, slapping Denzil's hand away, and plastering peanut butter on his bread. "I'm stuck until I have a date for Spy Wednesday. I could do with a bit more help, you know. It's no use sending you back to just any date. You only need to be one day late, and your old mate's got both feet in the grave."

"He won't be in a grave," said Denzil. "He'll be in a dragon's stomach."

"If we don't get you back on time, it won't

make any difference whether he's in a gizzard or a grave," said Adam grimly. "Either way, he'll be dead. You could show a bit more concern, instead of just floating around with your head in the clouds." He went back to the pantry to get some raisins, and Denzil slapped the other piece of bread on top, picked up the sandwich, and took a huge bite. Adam came back and started scattering raisins all over the worktop. "Hey – where'd my sandwich go?" he yelled.

"My gizzard," said Denzil, with his mouth full. "This is nice. Make me another one."

"Pig!" said Adam. "You'll get fat and split your fancy tights. I hope I'm around when it happens. I could do with a laugh out of you."

Denzil put out his skinny leg and admired the shiny pink material covering it. "They're still wrinkly," he said. "I've got some more room yet."

Theresa came home, dropped her schoolbag

on the table beside the computer, and gave Adam a smile and a quick kiss on the cheek. Denzil pulled a face. "Yuk," he said.

"Yuk, yourself," said Theresa. "Have you worked out when Spy Wednesday is yet?"

"Don't ask," said Adam.

Sam stamped in with Joplin in her arms. "This cat's going to obedience class," she announced, putting Joplin down. Joplin ran outside again. "He tried to eat Mrs Utherwise's bird," continued Sam. "He jumped right up onto his cage, and ripped out a tail feather. He doesn't do anything I say."

"Who's Mrs Utherwise?" asked Adam, starting to make another sandwich.

"That lady across the road," said Sam. "She moved in last week. She's got a cat with yellow eyes, and a black bird in a red cage."

"There's no one in that house," said Theresa. "It's still for sale. Another estate agent put up his sign this morning. I watched him, when I was leaving for school."

"Don't tease," said Sam. "You're as bad as Travis. Always trying to trick me."

"I'm not teasing," said Theresa. "The house is still empty, go and look."

"I just did," said Sam. "I was talking to her. She's put new curtains up, and planted some bushes in the garden. They smell nice. She gave me some lavender, look." She held out a tiny bunch of purple flowers and Denzil sniffed it.

"Mother Wyse grew that stuff," he said. "She had a cat with yellow eyes, and a black bird. Hers was a crow. We used to call her Old Battybird."

"Is that your friend with the broomstick?" asked Adam with an amused smile. "The witch?"

Denzil nodded. "She's not a very good witch, though," he said. "She's deaf. She's always getting words and things mixed up. Like she told me *I* was the one in danger. She said *I'd* be the one in a strange, big town on Spy Wednesday, and *I'd* be the one to get eaten by a dragon. Luckily, I worked out she must mean Valvasor."

Adam put down his sandwich and turned to look at Denzil. He looked at him hard, then said, very slowly and seriously: "But she was right, Denzil. You *are* in a big town. And it certainly is strange, to you. And since we don't know when it is, any day could be Spy Wednesday. The warning *was* for you."

Denzil's face went a peculiar grey colour, and he felt sick. "You got any dragons around here?" he asked.

Adam shook his head. "No. We don't have any dangerous animals. And anyway, we'll have you out of here by Spy Wednesday. It's probably weeks away, yet. Months, even."

"But what if it's not?" howled Denzil, wildly. "What if we don't find out when Spy Wednesday is until it's here? What if it comes, and the dragon comes, and I'm trampled and burnt and chomped up like a chicken in a fox's jaws? I'll be ruined!"

"No, you won't," said Adam, trying to sound calm. "It won't happen."

"You don't know that, Adam," said Theresa. "I think he's in terrible danger. Tomorrow's Wednesday. Tomorrow could be Spy Wednesday, for all we know."

Denzil screamed and collapsed on the floor. "Holy Jesus preserve me!" he wailed. "Mother Mary have mercy!"

Mr MacAllister came in, and Denzil flew into his arms. "Save me!" Denzil cried, sobbing. "It's almost Wednesday! And the dragon's on its way!"

Mr MacAllister looked puzzled, and stroked Denzil's hair. Denzil stopped wailing, but he shook uncontrollably, and his breath came in terrified gasps.

"Are you feeling sick?" asked Mr MacAllister, putting his hand on Denzil's forehead.

"You'd feel sick if a dragon was after you," said Sam. Her face was almost as white as Denzil's.

"What dragon?" asked her father, irritably. "Are you still going on about wizards and spells and dragons? I'm getting very tired of it."

"There isn't a dragon, Denzil," said Adam gently. "We don't have dragons here. The witch probably made a mistake. She probably meant you'd be stung by a wasp, or something like that."

"She didn't mean a wasp," whispered Denzil. "She told me what the dragon looked like. She said it was long and big and black, with one huge burning eye and terrible claws stretching out, and it's roaring and fast."

"You're perfectly safe, then," said Mr Mac-Allister, giving Denzil a hug. "We've got nothing like that here. Absolutely nothing."

"It could be something else big and fast," said Sam. "Like a lorry, or a bus. Maybe he'll get squashed by a bus."

Denzil howled, and Adam frowned at Sam. "Don't be stupid," said Theresa. "Lorries are nothing like dragons. It'll be an animal of some sort. Maybe a wild animal's going to escape from the zoo. A black panther, maybe, or a crocodile. I bet that's what's going to get him. A giant crocodile."

Denzil screamed and clung to Mr Mac-Allister's neck.

"That's not helping," scolded Adam. "If you carry on like that, the poor kid'll die of fright before anything gets him!" He lowered his voice, and tried to sound as calm as possible. "Denzil's already told us the witch makes mistakes. Denzil's probably not in any danger at all, not from a dragon or anything else. Spy Wednesday could be weeks away. We've probably got nothing at all to worry about."

"You might have nothing to worry about," said Mr MacAllister, "but I've got plenty. I've got a whole family going nuts. Now let's all start behaving like reasonable, intelligent people, and get some order back in our lives. Theresa, you start getting dinner. Your mother will be home soon, and the meat's not even thawed. Sam, you feed Joplin, then go and clean out Murgatroyd's cage. I could smell it from the garden. Adam, you take Denzil for a walk down to the dairy and buy some ice-cream for dessert."

"What are you going to do?" asked Adam. "Phone up the witch and check her story out?"

Mr MacAllister put Denzil down, and went over to the fridge. "I'm going to have a long, cold beer," he said, "and try to pretend that none of you are mad."

"Just as well you're an actor, then," grinned Adam. "You can pretend brilliantly." And he grasped Denzil's shoulder and marched him out the door.

Chapter 12

Tuesday

Dinner that night was one of the quietest the family had ever known. Mr Mac-Allister tried to tell a few jokes, but no one laughed. He left soon after the meal to go to work. Mrs MacAllister went out to a meeting, and Sam and Travis did the dishes. Theresa sat at the table with Denzil and Adam and did her homework while they stared blankly at the computer.

"I'm sorry, Denzil," sighed Adam, "but I can't do another thing until we have a date for Spy Wednesday. We can only hope it's still a week or two away."

Denzil nodded. He was still pale and jittery, and his green eyes had a haunted look about them. Every time he heard a loud noise outside, he jumped.

"I think we should hire a video, and forget all about Spy Wednesday," said Theresa brightly, putting down her pen. "We'll get something Denzil would like. What do you think, Adam?"

"Fine, so long as it's not anything startling," said Adam. "But I can't stay. I promised my sister she could borrow my car tonight. I'd better get back. I'll take the computer with me, and all the printout sheets. If you can think of any clues at all about Spy Wednesday, Denzil, get Theresa to give me a call." He turned the computer off and gave Denzil a tired smile. "Cheer up, kid. We'll work it out."

Theresa put away her homework, then helped Adam take the computer out to the car.

Travis went over to Denzil and sat down beside him. "Adam's right, Denzil," he said.

"We'll get your sums worked out, I promise. I feel it in my bones."

"I hope so," said Denzil gloomily. "If we don't, all I'll be feeling in *my* bones is dragon's teeth."

Travis grinned. "Adam knows what he's doing. He's a genius when it comes to physics and maths. He'll finish your calculations for you. Then you can write all the correct results into your spell, and – Abracadabra! – you'll be home."

"There's no such word in real magic," said Denzil, grumpily. "And the spell's no good, anyway, without the holy charm."

"What holy charm?" asked Travis.

"His medallion thing," said Sam, throwing a saucepan in the sink and splashing soapy water up the wall. "I hate washing saucepans, Travis. You come and do them."

But Travis was watching Denzil's face. "What charm?" he asked again.

"Noah's beard," said Denzil. "It was in a

special locket, gold on one side and silver on the other. The spell won't work unless I'm wearing it. Noah's beard's the real magic. The words in the spell just set all the power going, that's all. The beard's the real magic."

"He lost it," said Sam angrily, sloshing water all over the floor. "If he kept things tidy, he wouldn't lose them."

"I didn't lose it!" retorted Denzil. "And your treehouse was tidy! I tidied it, remember, while you gave the orders! Theresa messed it up again. She's the one who lost it, not me!"

"What have I lost?" asked Theresa, coming back into the room.

"My magic charm," said Denzil. "You lost it! It's all your fault!"

"Calm down, Denzil," said Travis. "I know you're worried about this dragon thing, but yelling and screaming isn't going to help. I'll go and get us a video, and some popcorn to eat while we watch it. But only if you behave yourself."

Half an hour later they were watching a medieval drama about a knight fighting to save a king's daughter. Denzil was enthralled, except when the princess got kissed, and then he made rude noises and spat popcorn everywhere. Sam was disgusted, with Denzil and with the film.

"You said it was a good one," she complained to Travis. "It's awful! Knights don't act like that."

"They do!" yelled Denzil.

"No, they don't!" cried Sam. "They ride white horses and live in castles."

"They're soldiers!" said Denzil. "Fighters. They're not milksops."

"That one is," sniffed Sam. "If I was a lady, I wouldn't want him slobbering all over me."

"You're not a lady," said Denzil, "and he wouldn't want to."

Before Sam could say any more, there was a knock on the back door, and she stamped off to answer it. It was Mrs Utherwise. She was smiling cheerfully, and held a plate of freshly baked hot cross buns, still steaming.

"Hello, dearie," she said to Sam. "I thought you might like these for supper. You and that young friend of yours. What's his name?"

"Joplin," said Sam.

"Jocelyn?" said Mrs Utherwise, screwing up her old face while she thought. "No, not him. That other one. Is he still here?"

"Oh, you mean Denzil," said Sam, taking the plate of hot cross buns. "Yes, he's still here. Thanks. These look great. We've been so worried about Denzil, we'd forgotten it's Easter this weekend. I hope Mum's remembered eggs and things. I love chocolate. I love Easter buns, too. Thanks. We'll eat them now."

Mrs Utherwise grabbed Sam's sleeve, and leaned close. "I know it's bad luck to bake them before Good Friday, dearie," she said in an urgent, croaky voice, "but I thought there'd be worse luck if I didn't. Tell Weasel they're Easter buns, won't you? Be sure to tell him. Tell him it's Maundy Thursday the day after tomorrow, then it's Good Friday. Don't forget."

"I will," promised Sam, smiling at Mrs Utherwise's worried face. "I'll tell him everything you said. Thank you."

Mrs Utherwise hobbled away, and Sam shut the door and took the buns into the lounge. "Look what I've got!" she announced. "They're from Mrs Utherwise across the road."

"Easter buns!" said Travis, surprised. "You know, with all this fuss over Denzil, I'd clean forgotten about Easter."

"Mrs Utherwise isn't real, and you know it," said Theresa. "Mum remembered after all. You should save those for the weekend, Sam."

"They're not for you, anyway," said Sam, huffily, and held out the plate towards Denzil. "Denzil? Have a hot cross bun."

Without taking his eyes off the television, Denzil helped himself to a bun, squashed it flat, and managed to stuff most of it into his mouth.

"They're from Mrs Utherwise," said Sam. "She said to tell you that it's Maundy Thursday the day after tomorrow."

"Mmm . . . they're good," mumbled Denzil, his eyes still on the knights. Suddenly he jumped up, screaming and choking, spraying soggy bun all over the lounge.

"Maundy Thursday?" he cried, wild eyed. "*Maundy Thursday*? She said it's Maundy Thursday *soon*?"

"Day after tomorrow," said Sam, sitting down and wondering what had upset him this time. "It's all right, Denzil. It's not Spy Wednesday."

"But it's Maundy Thursday!" Denzil wailed, hopping around in anguish. "Maundy Thursday's the day after Spy Wednesday! It's Spy Wednesday tomorrow! The Wednesday Judas spied on Jesus and told his enemies where he was, and they got him on Maundy Thursday and killed him on Good Friday! It's Spy Wednesday tomorrow! Oh, Lord, Jesus, Mary, I'm done for!"

Travis leapt up, raced out to the kitchen, and picked up the phone. Denzil collapsed in a quivering heap on the carpet. Sam and Theresa knelt on either side of him, not knowing what to say or do. They listened to Travis on the phone.

"Adam?" he said. "It's Travis. We've just found out that tomorrow's Spy Wednesday . . . it'd take too long to explain. But it is. Can you work it out? . . . What? . . . Yes . . . That's fine. We've got the spell here. Give us a ring as soon as you're finished, and we can write the correct numbers into the spell . . . Thanks. Bye."

Travis hung up and returned to the lounge. He knelt on the floor beside Denzil and lifted him up, gently. "It's all right, Denzil. Everything's going to be fine. Your spell's on the kitchen table with a pen, all ready to finish off with the correct numbers. Adam will call as soon as he's worked them out. You'll be home in your own little village in half an hour."

"No, I won't," whispered Denzil, clutching Travis's shirt. "I haven't got my charm."

"What charm?" asked Theresa.

"Noah's beard," moaned Denzil. "It's thousands of years old. It's holy and powerful, and the most precious thing Valvasor had."

"It's gold and silver," explained Sam. "Like a big round medallion. It's got Noah's beard inside."

"Oh." Theresa's face went white, then red. "I think I know where it is," she said, guiltily. "I had it. I gave it to Adam. I'm sorry, Sam. I found it in your treehouse. I thought, well, you're always taking stuff from my room, so I—"

But Travis was pushing Denzil into her arms, and racing back to the phone. He picked it up, then put it down again. He rushed into his room, and dragged on his leather jacket and motorbike boots. Looking up he saw his sisters and Denzil standing in the doorway. Denzil was transformed, joyful and excited. He looked as if all his Christmases had come at once – without the baths.

"I won't phone Adam again," said Travis,

zipping up his jacket, and winding a scarf around his neck. "He'll be in the middle of the calculations. He hasn't got his car now, anyway. I'll go on my bike, and pick the charm up. I'll bring the calculation results back, as well."

"Take me?" cried Sam and Theresa at the same time.

"Why don't we all go?" asked Theresa. "Take Mum's car."

"She's taken it, remember?" said Travis, rushing past them. He raced outside, and into the garage. Denzil hurried after him, followed closely by Sam and Theresa. It was getting dark outside now. The sky was a deep orange along the horizon, and stars winked in the velvet blue above. Travis wheeled out the motorbike and got on.

"Take me!" squealed Denzil, as Travis turned on the key and the headlight went on. Light streamed down the driveway ahead, and onto the road. "Take me!" howled Denzil again, jumping up and down with excitement.

Travis shook his head, and pulled on his helmet. "No, Denzil," he said, his voice sounding muffled and deep behind the black screen. "It's too dangerous."

"Please!" howled Denzil. "Please!"

Travis shook his head again, and kicked the bike into life. Denzil leapt on the back, and threw his arms around Travis's waist. He felt like a leech. Travis knew he'd never get him off. "Get the other helmet," he said to Theresa. "Hurry!"

She ran to the garage, got the helmet, and tried to put it on Denzil. Denzil shook his head violently. "Don't want it!" he yelled.

"You have to!" said Theresa. "Travis won't take you if you don't."

"No!"

"You'll look like a knight, with it on," said Sam. "A black knight. Like Travis."

Denzil kept still, and the helmet was fastened on. Theresa tapped Travis's shoulder. She couldn't see his face; it was hidden behind the shining black. "He's ready!" she said. Travis nodded and gave the thumbs up sign. He put the bike into gear, and moved off down the driveway. Denzil clung to him, trembling with terror and pure joy. Theresa and Sam saw them stop at the kerb, waiting for a passing car; then the bike turned into the road, and roared off.

Theresa looked at her watch, and put her arm around Sam's neck. "Well, we've got four hours until midnight," she said, as they went inside to wait. "Four hours till Spy Wednesday."

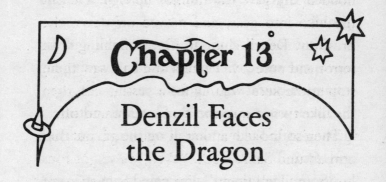

Chapter 13°

Denzil Faces the Dragon

Theresa made a cup of coffee for herself and a milkshake for Sam, then sat down at the kitchen table. She stared absent-mindedly at Denzil's spell.

"Don't read that," said Sam, turning the spell over. "It might make you disappear."

Theresa smiled. "I thought you wanted me to disappear," she said, "so you can have my room. Anyway, that spell's not really magic."

"Yes it is," said Sam.

"It isn't. Adam said it's all scientific. It's to do with quantum energy, and the reorganization of matter, and all that. He said Denzil's a thousand years ahead of his time. A scientific genius."

"I think he's a wizard," said Sam, gulping down the rest of her milkshake and wiping her creamy moustache on her sleeve.

There was a noise on the driveway outside, a grating sound like a footfall on the gravel. Both girls froze.

"Someone's there!" whispered Sam, her eyes like saucers. "A prowler! Or maybe it's the dragon!"

"I knew we should have got a dog," whispered Theresa. "Don't worry, Sis. I'll fix him." Without a sound she put down her coffee cup then moved back her chair and stood up. She picked up a heavy saucepan from the kitchen bench, and opened the back door. It was almost dark outside now. Theresa switched on the back porch light and moved out onto the step. There was no one there. She checked the driveway. There was something dark on the gravel, something round and gleaming black. Theresa approached it cautiously, then laughed and picked it up.

"It's Denzil's helmet!" she called back to Sam, who was standing white-faced in the doorway. "He sent it back!" She put the helmet in the garage, then went back inside. "Travis will be furious· when he notices," she said, sitting down again. "It's illegal to ride without a helmet. I hope a cop doesn't see them. Travis'll be fined."

"He goes so fast a cop couldn't catch him," said Sam.

Theresa's eyebrows rose. "Oh? And how would you know, Sam?" she asked. "You're not allowed on a motorbike . . ."

Sam shot her a guilty look and shrugged.

"You're as bad as Denzil," said Theresa. She hesitated, then said slowly, "Sam, I'm sorry I messed up your treehouse the other day. When I thought you'd been into my things again, just after I told you not to, I got really mad. I didn't know it was Denzil. I'm sorry. I'll paint your walls again and cover up the things I wrote. I'll paint them any colour you want. And I'll make new curtains to match."

Sam's face lit up. "Rainbow walls? Can I have rainbow walls? And stars on the ceiling? And rainbow curtains like Janey's got?"

Theresa sighed, and grinned. "You certainly make things difficult, Sis. But all right."

Sam jumped up and hugged Theresa's neck. "Thanks! This weekend?"

"This weekend," promised Theresa. "I'll need something to do, anyway. Adam's got a special course to go to at the university. He'll be busy all weekend."

"He's brainy, isn't he?" said Sam. "Dad said so, the other night. He said he's really impressed with Adam, and the way he talks about quadrangle energy and all that stuff."

"Quantum energy," smiled Theresa. "Did Dad really say that? That he's impressed with Adam? Wow! Miracles do happen!"

They heard a motorbike roaring up the road, and Sam jumped up. But it went on past, and she sat down again. Theresa glanced at her watch. "They'll be back soon," she said. "It only takes five minutes to get to Adam's on a bike. Three minutes for Travis. They'll be back before quarter past eight, I bet."

But they weren't back by quarter past eight, or by nine o'clock. At quarter past nine Theresa phoned Adam.

"Hi, Theresa," he answered. "Has Denzil gone then?"

"No . . . have they been to your place?" asked Theresa.

"They left here nearly an hour ago," said Adam. "They had all the calculations, and the charm. Everything's perfect. I thought they'd have been home, finished the spell, and it'd be over by now."

"They haven't come back," said Theresa in a small voice. "Oh, Adam. What's happened to them?"

Adam was silent.

"Adam?" she wailed. "I'm scared! What if they've had an accident?"

"No . . . they wouldn't have. Not Travis," said Adam, wishing he didn't sound so worried. "He's far too good on a bike. Don't worry, Theresa. They'll turn up. Call me when they do."

Theresa hung up, and went back to Sam. "They left Adam's nearly an hour ago," she said.

Sam chewed her nails and said nothing.

Theresa shrugged, and tried to smile. "Travis is probably showing him around the city," she said, brightly. "Denzil hasn't seen a city before, has he?"

"No," said Sam, gloomily. "He hasn't been chased by a dragon before, either."

"Don't worry, Sis," said Theresa. "You go and get ready for bed. I bet they're home before you've got your pyjamas on."

*   *   *

But at eleven o'clock Travis and Denzil still weren't home. At eleven-fifteen Mrs MacAllister got home from her meeting, and soon afterwards Mr MacAllister arrived home from work. Mrs MacAllister made hot drinks, but no one wanted them. The phone went, and Mr MacAllister rushed to answer it. It was Adam, wondering what was happening. Mr MacAllister talked to him for a while, then hung up. Sam started to look tired and pale, but no one told her to go to bed. Then, at ten minutes to midnight, they heard Travis's bike come up the drive. They all rushed outside, talking and laughing with relief. But Travis was getting off his bike slowly, as if he were desperately tired – and he was alone.

"Where's Denzil?" cried Sam, pulling on Travis's hand, and feeling how cold he was. "Where is he?"

Travis took off his helmet, and they saw that his face was white and strained. "I've lost him," he said. "I've been looking for him for hours. He's gone."

They gazed at him, dumbfounded. Travis sighed heavily, and went inside. The rest of the family followed, silent and shocked. In the kitchen, Travis unzipped his leather jacket and took out a sheaf of papers. Carefully he unrolled them and put them on the table beside the spell. "The calculations," he said. Then he took the charm out of an inside pocket, and placed it on the spell. It lay there under the kitchen light, the silver moon smooth and shining and filled with ancient power. Travis sat down, leaned his elbows on the table, and buried his face in his hands.

"I lost him," he said huskily. "I was chased by a cop. I didn't even know he was following me, until his siren started. Man, those things make a noise when they're right next to you! Anyway, I pulled over, and then I realized Denzil was gone. He must have been frightened by the siren and flashing lights. I guess he turned himself into a bird or something, and flew off. Anyway, he wasn't there."

Mr MacAllister swore, furiously. "I suppose you were speeding again!" he said. "You'll never learn, will you? You could've killed the kid, as well as yourself! Well, I hope you lose your licence this time. It might teach you a lesson."

"I wasn't speeding, Dad," objected Travis. "I was being extra careful. The last thing I wanted was to have an accident or get pulled up by the police. It was Denzil. The stupid kid took his helmet off. I don't know how, but he did. I noticed in the rear-view mirror that he didn't have it on any more, but there was nothing I could do about it. And that's why we got stopped. We were nearly home."

"Well, what happened then?" asked Theresa. "What did the policeman say, when he saw your pillion passenger sprout wings and take off?"

"He didn't see him fly off," said Travis. "Neither did I. Denzil just vanished. The officer was quite apologetic, actually. He said he was sure he'd seen a pillion rider on my bike, without a helmet. He even described Denzil, right down to the pink tights. I denied everything, of course. I could hardly say I'd been riding with a wizard, and he turned into a bird and flew off! The cop would have thought I was drunk. So I pretended I didn't know anything.

"Then the policeman said he was sorry, he must have made a mistake. The poor chap must have thought he was going mad. I felt sorry for him. After he went, I spent ages looking for Denzil. All up and down the road, and then around the block. I even looked in people's gardens, calling him. In the end I must have searched every road in the city. I even went to the hospital, to see if he'd been taken there. I don't know where he is. He's gone. I'm sorry."

"It's not your fault," said Sam, winding her arm around his neck. "He's probably just up a tree somewhere, or flying around looking for our house."

"I hope he keeps an eye out for power lines," said Mrs MacAllister nervously.

"I hope he *is* a bird, and not a hedgehog," said Theresa. "Wouldn't it be awful if he was on the road somewhere, and—"

"I think I'll make us all a hot drink," cut in Mrs MacAllister quickly. "I think we might have a long night ahead of us."

"I don't want anything," said Sam. "I feel sick."

Travis looked at his watch. "It's after midnight," he said. "It's Spy Wednesday now."

They were all silent, dismayed. They stared at the calculations and the spell and the shining charm, lying there waiting.

"There must be something we can do," muttered Mr MacAllister, after a while. "I don't believe in all this Spy Wednesday and dragon and wizard stuff, but that kid out there is lost. Anything could happen to him. There must be something we can do."

"We could go out and look for the dragon,

and stop it catching him," suggested Sam.

"There isn't a dragon," said Theresa impatiently. "I told you. It'll be an escaped crocodile or something from the zoo."

"A crocodile hasn't got one blazing eye," said Sam. "Denzil said the dragon Mother Wyse warned him about has one blazing gold eye and huge claws, and it's long and black and fast, and it roars. A crocodile doesn't roar. I think it's a bus or a truck."

"Maybe Sam's got a point," said Travis, frowning as he thought. "What if Denzil's witch saw something in our world – something she'd never seen before – and she didn't know what to call it? If it had headlights, wouldn't she call them blazing yellow eyes? If it made a noise and moved, wouldn't she think it was alive? And if it was long and huge and very fast, wouldn't she think it was a terrible kind of animal? Wouldn't she call it a dragon?"

"That's what I've been trying to tell you!" yelled Sam. "She saw a bus, or a lorry!"

"Buses and lorries haven't got claws," said Theresa. "And they've got two headlights, not one. I think you're barking up the wrong tree. If someone from the Middle Ages saw a crocodile, they'd call that a dragon. It's an animal."

"No, it's not," insisted Sam, screwing up her eyes and thinking hard. She tried to imagine something roaring and dark and long. A lorry with a trailer, maybe? It had to be long. With claws. A train, perhaps. A train was long, with one blazing light, and a roar. A train moved fast, and raced along lines that looked like long shining . . .

"A train!" she shrieked, jumping up and down. "A train has one blazing eye and a roar and rails like long claws! It's a train!"

"Into the car!" cried Mr MacAllister. "Quickly! We'll check the railway station, and then every intersection where lines are. Move!"

Sam didn't know her father could drive so fast. The car zoomed down the dark streets; charged, hooting madly, past delivery trucks;

hurtled, tyres squealing, around corners; and screeched to a halt outside the railway station. They flung open the car doors and all rushed through the main gates to the station. Light blazed everywhere. A few people wandered around, waiting for a late train. The lines were empty.

"He must be somewhere else," said Mrs MacAllister, as they ran back to the car and got in. "We'll check all the intersections, and every place in this city where railway lines are."

For over an hour they drove, searching, but they saw no sign of Denzil. They ended up in a huge industrial area full of warehouses, sheds and factories, and criss-crossed by railway lines. As they drove towards the first set of lines, the red lights of the barrier started flashing, and the black and white wooden barrier came down. Mr MacAllister stopped the car to wait, his fingers drumming impatiently on the steering-wheel. They could hear the train coming, a low rumble at first, a long way off; then nearer.

They heard its whistle, a faint warning sound in the vast night. Sam looked down across the barrier at the dark road and the ghostly buildings on the other side. A small figure ran out, and Sam leaned forward, staring.

"Look! It's Denzil!" she said.

They all looked in the direction of her pointing finger but the figure disappeared into the shadows. Then it came out again, closer this time, and ran into the pale edge of the beams from the car lights.

"It is Denzil!" cried Sam. She threw open the car door. "Denzil!" she screamed. Travis grabbed her, trying to stop her, to keep her quiet – but it was too late. Denzil had heard. He looked up and started running towards them, his legs flashing bright pink in the car headlights. The silk dressing-gown flapped about him like black wings and his face was white. He seemed confused, and he held his hands up in front of his eyes.

Travis was out of the car, and pushing Sam

behind him. "Don't move!" he hissed. "He's blinded by the lights. Turn them off, Dad." He ran to the barrier, and called out to Denzil: "Denzil! It's me, Travis. Stay where you are. Don't come any closer. Stay there!"

Denzil smiled, and rushed up to the opposite barrier, on the other side of the lines. "Travis? I'm safe then!"

"No!" shouted Travis. "Stay there! There's a train coming!" But the warning was lost in the train's whistle, piercing and close. Terrified, and more confused than ever, Denzil bent and crawled under the barrier. He hadn't seen the train. He stood on the line bewildered, and rubbed his eyes again.

"Are you still there, Travis?" he called. Then he heard the rumbling, the thunder and roar coming closer and closer; heard the clatter and scream of some huge thing rushing towards him; realized, with terror, that he stood between its shining claws; and looked up in those last seconds and saw the dragon's eye. He stood frozen with fear and awe. Then something hit him, knocking the breath out of him, and he felt himself crushed tight, and rolled over and over on the hard ground. The dragon thundered and boomed beside him, and the whole world shook.

Then, suddenly, it was quiet. Denzil lay rigid, panting with terror, still clutched tightly in someone's arms, his ears still ringing with the dragon's roar. Slowly, he opened his eyes. He saw a hairy chest, a torn blue shirt, and a leather jacket. He looked up further, and saw Travis's face.

Travis gave him a pale grin. "Well, you survived, Denzil," he said, in a shaky voice. "I think you just met your dragon, and lived."

Denzil struggled free, stood up, and dusted off his pink tights. His face was white and hurt, and he looked angry. "You said there weren't any dragons here!" he cried. "You lied, Travis! You all lied!"

Travis stood up and put his arms around

Denzil's shoulders. "We didn't lie," he said, gently. "That wasn't really a dragon. It was a train."

Mr MacAllister came rushing over, and threw his arms around them. "God – I thought you'd both been killed!" he said, in a strange hoarse voice. Mrs MacAllister and the girls joined in the hug, white-faced, but smiling with relief.

Denzil wrenched himself free, and stood a little way apart, his shoulders hunched, his green eyes flashing. "You said there weren't any dragons!" he shouted. "And there was one, just like Mother Wyse said!"

Mr MacAllister tried to laugh, and failed. "What are you talking about, Denzil?" he asked. "That was a train. You were nearly run over by a train."

"It was a dragon!" cried Denzil, furious. "Are you all dumb or something? It was a dragon, all long and black and roaring, with a blazing yellow eye and long claws!"

"Look," said Sam, bending down and pointing to the railway lines. "The claws are still here. They're railway lines, Denzil. The train's wheels run on them, and can't go anywhere except on these lines. It wasn't a dragon, it was a train, a vehicle like a car or a bus. But if this is what Mother Wyse saw in her dream, it would look like a dragon to her."

Denzil crouched beside her and touched the line, cautiously. "It was a *train*?" he asked, still not totally convinced. "Mother Wyse saw a train?"

Sam smiled. "A train, Denzil. Not a dragon at all. A train. And you've seen it, and lived. You're all right. The danger's over now. You can go home."

Denzil's face broke into a huge smile. "Wow!" he breathed, amazed. "Wait 'til I tell old Battybird! All those roaring beasts that live in caves, all those dragons the knights fight – they're all trains! Wow!"

He stood up again, shaking his head in

wonder, amazed at the discovery and his own stupendous wisdom.

Trying hard not to laugh, Sam took Denzil back to the car. The others followed, smiling, and no one had the heart to put Denzil right.

Chapter 14

The Witch's Secret

Denzil forgot he wasn't using his quill pen and a bottle of ink, and dipped his pen in his hot chocolate. He then dripped the drink all over the spell, which smudged the ink. He wrote in some more numbers and then leaned back, satisfied.

"I've finished!" he said, with a triumphant smile.

"Terrific!" said Sam, peering over his shoulder at the smudged ink and the blurred words. She tried not to read them, but she couldn't help noticing he'd spelt "tomorrow" wrong.

"Don't look at that," said her father, putting his hands on her shoulders and turning her away. "That's magic, remember. I don't want you vanishing into the Middle Ages. The only place you're allowed to vanish to is into bed."

"I want to see Denzil go, first," Sam protested. "You're ready now, aren't you, Denzil?"

Denzil pushed back his chair, stood up, and picked up the spell. He looked down at the charm, glinting silver and gold against the black silk. "I suppose you want your clothes back," he said to Travis and Theresa, sadly.

They both shook their heads. "Keep them," said Theresa smiling. "I'll be honoured to know that my ballet tights are dancing their way through medieval England."

"I don't dance," said Denzil, "I fly."

"I'll imagine a falcon with pink satin legs, then," said Theresa.

Denzil went outside to the lawn and the MacAllisters gathered around him, silent, excited . . . and sad. Sam stood close to Travis, and he slipped his arm around her.

Denzil looked at them all, and tried to appear cheerful. "I'll miss all of you," he said. "It was fun at your manor hall. Except for the baths."

"You only had three," said Sam.

Denzil grinned. "I won't need another one for three years then," he said. "By then I'll be fourteen. Grown up. I'll be a fantastic wizard by then. I'll never get my sums wrong and I'll be able to come and visit you whenever I like."

"That will be wonderful," said Mrs Mac-Allister, warmly. "You'll always be welcome, Denzil."

Mr MacAllister cleared his throat. "Well . . . give us a call first, Denzil," he said. "Just to make sure we're not watching anything exciting on TV."

Denzil nodded. "I'll tell Valvasor to make us a telephone," he said. "I'll never forget the galaxy," he added, "or you playing the court jester." He went over to Sam and for a few moments stood awkwardly in front of her. Then, very solemnly, he bowed. "Thank you for helping me, lady," he said.

She smiled and gave him a kiss on the cheek. For a few seconds, Denzil was stunned; then he blushed scarlet, and tried not to look pleased. He glanced at Travis, and smiled shyly. "Thank you for saving me from the train," he said. "You're the bravest knight I know."

"You're welcome," said Travis, gravely. "You're the best and bravest wizard I know. It was an honour to help."

Denzil blushed again. "I'm not really all that brave."

"I think you are," smiled Travis. "You wouldn't get me travelling through seven centuries on nothing but a spell and a magic charm."

Denzil flashed them all a brilliant smile, and went to stand a short distance away. They watched as he lifted the spell high, and they saw him turn it a little, so that the light from the house fell on the words. Sam wanted to run and stand there with him, but she felt Travis's hand warm and strong on her shoulder, and she stayed. She listened as Denzil started chanting the spell; listened to his singsong voice rise and soar in the still night air; listened to the strong, shining, spell-spinning words, and heard their force and enchantment and all their power.

And while she listened, she watched Denzil's face. It glowed. Strange lights seemed to shine about him, and she thought she heard quiet voices, and people singing. She saw his whole body quiver with incredible light, radiant and pure; and then she saw him fade slowly, like a figure in a dream. Slowly, slowly he faded, still chanting the magic; and then, when he was almost gone, he looked at her and smiled and lifted his hand and waved. Then he vanished.

Sam pressed her face into Travis's leather jacket, and wept. "He was my best stray," she said.

"I know," said Travis, giving her a hug, and

leading her back inside. "But he was always a stray, Sam, never our own. He had to go back to where he belonged. He could only stay with us for a short time."

Sam wiped her eyes and looked up. "But it was a terrific time, wasn't it?" she said. "The best time ever."

"It certainly was," smiled Travis.

Mrs MacAllister blew her nose, and then looked at her watch. "Talking of time," she said, "it's almost two in the morning. Time you were in bed, Samantha."

Sam yawned. "I'll find Joplin, first," she said. "I want him to sleep with me tonight."

She found Joplin in the lounge, crouched over the plate of hot cross buns on the floor. "I'd forgotten about those," said Sam, picking Joplin up. "Luckily you've left some. I'll have them for breakfast."

Travis came in. He bent over the plate of buns for a moment or two, then poked one with his finger. He pulled it away again, quickly.

"They're still hot!" he cried, astounded. "How can they possibly still be hot? They've been sitting here for hours!" He gave Sam a long, questioning look. "Where did you get those buns?" he asked.

"From Mrs Utherwise," said Sam, stifling another yawn. "That old lady in the house across the road."

"There isn't anyone in that house," said Travis, puzzled. "It's still for sale." He opened the patio door of the lounge, and went out across the lawn and stood by the front gate. He was still holding the plate of buns, and the steam from them rose in the night air, and smelled delicious.

Sam stood beside Travis, still holding Joplin in her arms. Joplin strained towards the buns and licked the rim of the plate.

"There's no one there," said Travis. "There never has been."

"Yes, there is," said Sam impatiently, pulling Joplin away and wiping the crumbs off his face.

She glanced up and pointed across the road. "See? There's the red . . ." Her voice trailed off in astonishment. The red birdcage, the pot plants, the new curtains in the windows – all were gone. The garden, yesterday so carefully weeded and dug and planted with lavender, now grew tall weeds, a tangled jungle of dandelions, deadly nightshade, and long uncut grass. By the front gate, white and ghostly in the moonlight, was a huge FOR SALE sign, exactly as it had been before. A new sign was beside it.

Sam stared, saying nothing.

"Are you sure she was there?" Travis looked anxiously into Sam's white face. "Are you really sure?"

"Of course she was there," said Sam. "I visited her. I got the duck egg from her. And she gave me the hot cross buns."

"The buns that never got cold," murmured Travis, in a wondering voice. "What was her name, Sam? Utherwise? Mrs Utherwise?"

"Yes," said Sam, puzzled. "Mrs Utherwise.

She moved in a week ago. About the same time Denzil arrived." Suddenly her eyes grew round, and her face went red with excitement. "Travis! Do you think she had something to do with Denzil? With his being here? Do you think she was magic, too?"

Travis nodded. "That witch who warned Denzil about the dragon – her name was Mother Wyse. It sounds suspiciously like Utherwise, doesn't it?"

"And Mother Wyse had a black bird!" cried Sam. "And she couldn't hear very well. Denzil told me. Mrs Utherwise couldn't hear very well, either. When I asked her for an egg, she thought I asked for a nutmeg. And she called Denzil 'Weasel' all the time. Oh, Travis! Do you think. . . ?"

Travis nodded, grinning, and tore a piece off a bun that Joplin hadn't chewed. He ate it slowly, thoughtfully, while he looked at the empty house across the road.

Sam slipped her hand around Travis's arm.

"Do you think we'll ever see her again?" she asked. "Or Denzil?"

Travis nodded again, and ate another piece of bun. "We'll see Denzil again, for sure," he said. "On the way home tonight, in the car, he told me he'd like to see the way we celebrate Christmas. Or, if he can't make it for Christmas, he'll try Michaelmas, or Plough Monday, or Mothering Sunday."

"Oh, no!" groaned Sam, and Travis gave her a wink.

"Only joking," he laughed.

Denzil hitched up his pink tights, smoothed down his silk dressing-gown, and banged loudly on Mother Wyse's door.

"Come in!" she called, cheerily, and he pushed open the door and went in. Mother Wyse was sitting by the firepit, spinning. "Hello, Weasel," she croaked, smiling her one-tooth smile. "Well, well! Don't you look handsome, in your new clothes! I'm glad you've called. I've got some fresh honeycomb for you. But you mustn't eat it all before Valvasor comes home. You must leave some for him."

"Thanks," said Denzil. He pulled up a small stool and sat down beside her. She went on spinning, but her shrewd eyes were fixed on Denzil's face.

"So, Spy Wednesday has come and gone, and you're still alive," she said. "I'm pleased to see it, Weasel. Very pleased."

"You were wrong," said Denzil. "It wasn't a dragon. It was a train. It was long and black and roaring, like you said, but it was a train."

"Oh dear. I'm not usually wrong," murmured Mother Wyse, stopping her spinning, and folding her gnarled hands on her white apron. "A brain, you say. Oh dear. How awful."

"No. A train!" shouted Denzil. "It's a vehicle. It shoots along a shining line thing, faster than an arrow. I saw it. It was fantastic!"

"And you weren't afraid?" asked Mother Wyse, admiringly.

"Heavens, no!" said Denzil, puffing out his chest. "I've seen more amazing things than trains. I've been away. A long, long way away. I've seen things you wouldn't dream about. I've seen things called telephones that munch up people's voices and squash them along tiny lines you can't see, and spit them out in other people's ears. I've seen things called bulbs, that go on at night – flash! – brighter than the sun, and then go off again, quicker than a wink. I've even had a bath! Three baths, in fact! Have you ever heard of anything so ridiculous? I could have washed all my skin off! I reckon they stopped just in time!

"And I've been on – Oh, Mother Wyse, you'll never believe this – I've been on a motor-bike! Roaring like a wild beast, it was, and it was cold – cold as the devil – on its way back, and we fairly flew. I've never been so fast, in all my life! And we had to wear helmets like knights, in case we met other knights on raging beasts, and banged into them. But I took mine off. Oh, it was marvellous!" He sighed blissfully, remembering.

Then he frowned. "At least, it *was* marvellous, until something screamed in my ear, and I got such a fright I flew off. That's when I got lost, and saw the train."

"You have had an exciting time," murmured Mother Wyse, smiling faintly.

"But that's not the best of it," said Denzil, moving to the edge of his stool and gripping her arm. "I saw the most wonderful thing God ever made. I saw the galaxy."

And for the next two hours, he told her about it. Mother Wyse listened, sometimes asking him to repeat things, sometimes gasping with astonishment, nodding wisely or hiding an amused smile. When he had finished, she got up and threw some more wood on her fire. She wrapped some honeycomb in a clean cloth and gave it to him.

"Thank you for coming, Weasel," she said, seeing him off at the door. "You have told me great and wondrous things today."

Denzil grinned, and put the honeycomb in his pocket. "I wish you could have seen it all," he said, walking away backwards, his shampooed hair gleaming in the sun. "I wish you could go to where I've been. You'd love it, Mother Wyse."

Mother Wyse nodded. "I'm sure I would, Weasel. I'm sure I would."

And she gave him a knowing, secret smile, and closed the door.